3

SUGAR CREEK GANG
The WINTER
RESCUE

Paul Hutchens

MOODY PUBLISHERS
CHICAGO

Original Title: *Further Adventures of the Sugar Creek Gang*

ISBN: 978-0-8024-7007-2
Printed by Bethany Press in Bloomington, MN – 12/2009

We hope you enjoy this book from Moody Publishers.
Our goal is to provide high-quality, thought-provoking
books and products that connect truth to your real needs
and challenges. For more information on other books
and products written and produced from a biblical per-
spective, go to www.moodypublishers.com or write to:

Moody Publishers
820 N. LaSalle Boulevard
Chicago, IL 60610

13 15 17 19 20 18 16 14 12

Printed in the United States of America

PREFACE

Hi—from a member of the Sugar Creek Gang!

It's just that I don't know which one I am. When I was good, I was Little Jim. When I did bad things—well, sometimes I was Bill Collins or even mischievous Poetry.

You see, I am the daughter of Paul Hutchens, and I spent many an hour listening to him read his manuscript as far as he had written it that particular day. I went along to the north woods of Minnesota, to Colorado, and to the various other places he would go to find something different for the Gang to do.

Now the years have passed—more than fifty, actually. My father is in heaven, but the Gang goes on. All thirty-six books are still in print and now are being updated for today's readers with input from my five children, who also span the decades from the '50s to the '70s.

The real Sugar Creek is in Indiana, and my father and his six brothers were the original Gang. But the idea of the books and their ministry were and are the Lord's. It is He who keeps the Gang going.

PAULINE HUTCHENS WILSON

The *Sugar Creek Gang* Series:

1

Beginning to write a story is something like diving under a cold shower—or taking the first plunge into Sugar Creek when the water's cold. It's hard to get started. But after I'm in, paragraph deep, and my thoughts are splashing around a little, it certainly feels great. My words go swimming and diving and having a good time —in ink, of course, because I always use a pen when I write.

So, hurrah! Here I am, already started, trudgening along faster than anything on a brand new Sugar Creek Gang story. Does it ever feel good to be writing again!

In just a minute I'll explain what I mean by "trudgening." That is, I'll explain it when I'm telling you about the last time our gang went in swimming before school started that fall.

That was kind of a sad day for us—that last Saturday. Especially for Little Jim, and I'll have to tell you about it even though I don't like to write about sad things.

Hm, I wonder how many miles the point of a boy's pen travels while he's writing a long story like this one's going to be. Hundreds and hundreds of miles, I guess, although I never figured it up. Not liking arithmetic very well is the main reason.

Well, none of us boys wanted school to begin, even though we knew every boy ought to have an education if he wanted to amount to anything. But at last that wonderful summer was over, and we knew there wasn't any way to get out of it. Going to school is like starting to swim too. After you get in, it's fun, and it's good for you. It washes all the ignorance off a boy and makes him feel good.

It was Saturday, the last Saturday of our summer, and it was noon at our house. I took the last bite of my three-cornered piece of blackberry pie and chewed it as long as I could because it tasted so good I hated to swallow it. Then I looked across the table at my dad's bushy blackish-red eyebrows to see if he was going to say no when I asked him if I could go swimming.

Charlotte Ann, my three-month-old, black-haired baby sister, was in her blue-and-white bassinet, kind of half lying down and half sitting up like a baby bird in a nest full of pillows. She was smiling as if she was happier than anything and was gurgling and drooling, which means she was making bubbles of saliva tumble out of her soft little lips. And her arms and legs were going like four windmills whirling all at once. Her pretty little ears looked like the halves of dried peaches, which somebody had glued onto the side of her head.

She's getting prettier all the time, I thought. *If only she doesn't get red hair like mine.* I could see that someday maybe there'd be freckles on her nose, and I felt sorry for her because I had freckles myself and didn't like them. In fact, there were freckles all over my face.

Dad's big eyebrows were halfway between up and down, and Mom was busy eating her pie and smiling back at Charlotte Ann. In fact, Dad was looking at Charlotte Ann too, as if Bill Collins—that's my name—wasn't even important anymore. I had had to take second place at our house ever since Charlotte Ann was born. That's what a boy has to do when a new baby comes to his house to live.

I sighed, thinking about how hot it was and looking over the top of a stack of dirty dishes in the sink by the window. I was wishing I was outdoors running through the woods toward the spring, where I knew Dragonfly, Poetry, Circus, Big Jim, and Little Jim would be waiting for me and where old Sugar Creek would be almost screaming for us to come and jump into it.

The creek wanted to prove to us its water was still warm enough to swim in, even if it was going to be fall pretty soon. Then it would be winter, and Sugar Creek would have a cold, sad face until the spring rains came and washed it again and the sun melted its ice coat and made it happy. Say, if I were old Sugar Creek, about the only time I could ever be happy would be when a gang of boys was swimming in my warm, sparkling water.

I looked away from the window without seeing the dishes and was looking at the little Scottish terrier design on Charlotte Ann's bassinet when I said, "Look at her wave her arms and legs, Dad! I'll bet she could swim without even having to learn how."

My dad could read my thoughts just like I could read an electric sign on a city store. You should have seen his big eyebrows drop like a grassy ledge caving in along Sugar Creek. "Those aren't swimming movements," he said, taking a last bite of pie. "Those are movements a boy's hands make when he is doing the dishes."

That's why I was the last one of our gang to get to the spring that day.

It seemed to take almost an hour to wash those dishes. While I was doing them, I looked down at Charlotte Ann, who was still making spit bubbles. Her lips were like two red rose petals all wet with dew, and I thought, *Go on, little innocent child, and have your play! Someday you'll grow up, and then you'll have to work!* And for a minute I was mad at her for not growing faster.

But pretty soon the dishes were all done and set away, and I was feeling happy again. I made a dive for my straw hat, which was on the floor in a corner where I wasn't supposed to put it. Mom always wanted me to hang it up. A jiffy later I was outside, my bare feet carrying me lickety-sizzle down the path through the woods to the spring.

I tell you, it was great to be with the gang again. Maybe I'd better tell you about our gang just in case you may not have read my other Sugar Creek Gang stories—although it seems everybody in the world ought to know about us, with all the newspaper publicity we got after Little Jim killed that fierce old mother bear. If he hadn't, she might have ripped him all to pieces with her horrible teeth and claws or maybe hugged him to death the way bears do.

Well, this was our gang: Big Jim, our leader, who was so big he had actually shaved his fuzzy mustache once and who had been a Scout; Little Jim, a great little guy with blue eyes like Charlotte Ann's and the best Christian in the world; Circus, our acrobat, who right that very minute was sitting on the first limb of a maple sapling looking like a chimpanzee; Poetry, who was short and globular—which means "round, like a globe"—and who knew 101 poems by heart; Dragonfly, whose eyes were very large like a dragonfly's eyes—he could see better than the rest of us; and me, Bill Collins.

The new member of our gang was there too, Little Jim's pet bear, the little black baby bear whose savage mother got killed in my last story. That brown-nosed bear was the cutest, most awkward little fellow you ever saw. He could already do a half dozen tricks. We had named him Triangle because there was a three-cornered white spot on his chest like black baby bears sometimes have.

Little Jim had put a new leather collar on Triangle's neck with the word *Triangle* engraved on it. And Little Jim's favorite Bible verse was right below that: "Train up a child in the way he should go, even when he is old he will not depart from it."

I never saw anybody in my life who was a better Christian than Little Jim, and he wasn't ashamed of being one either. In fact, he was proud of it.

Poetry had made up a good poem about Triangle, which started like this:

Black little, bad little, brown-nosed bear,
Frowzy little fellow with a tail that isn't there.

Bears really don't have tails except for a stubby little stump that looks kind of like a dog's tail that has been cut off. Only Triangle's tail didn't stand straight up the way a tail does on a happy dog. It hung down the way a sheep's tail does.

No girls belonged to our gang. None of us boys liked girls very well. Girls are such funny things, always scared of mice and screaming whenever they see a spider or something. Circus *did* have a kind of nice ordinary-looking sister whom I'd made up my mind I was going to kill a spider for as soon as I got a chance—which I didn't get until school started that fall.

But we decided to let Little Jim's bear belong. Bears aren't afraid of mice. They even eat them. Triangle liked mice, frogs, fish, ants, bees and their honey, blackberry pie, and things like that. We couldn't let him eat too much honey or other sweet things at one time, though, or he'd have gotten sick.

You should have seen that little fellow swim! He was as playful as a kitten in the water. And he was only about three times as big as a big tomcat, although he was growing fast.

Well, there we were, all of us barefoot, knowing that next Monday we'd have to wear shoes all day at school and feeling sad because of it. All of a sudden, Circus—who, as I told you, was sitting on the first limb of a maple sapling—let out a war whoop, slid down the tree, and started running toward the swimming hole, yelling back over his shoulder, "Last one in's a bear's tail!"

In less than a jiffy all the gang was running right after him as fast as they could go—all except Little Jim and Triangle and me. That mischievous little rascal of a bear had evidently made up his mind he didn't want to go in swimming, because he wouldn't even get up when Little Jim told him to. He just lay there in the sun as though he was too lazy or sleepy to move.

I caught hold of the chain that was fastened to his collar, and both of us pulled and scolded until Triangle growled a disgusted sort of growl and whined lazily. That made Little Jim decide to give him a switching with a little willow switch, which is what you have to do with baby bears when they won't obey you.

That switching helped a little, like punishment does a boy for a while, and soon we were on our way to the swimming hole. I noticed when we were half pulling the little bear along behind us that the collar around his neck was a bit too loose and maybe we'd better tighten it another notch. But Little Jim said he thought that'd be too tight and might choke Triangle. Besides, the collar was locked on, and the key was at Little Jim's house almost a quarter of a mile away.

Then we were at the swimming hole. Because Triangle was still stubborn and didn't want to go into the water and was cross when we threw him in and wouldn't do any of his tricks for us, Little Jim decided to tie him to an ash sapling up on the bank.

"Smarty," Little Jim said. "I'm going to tie you up behind this big stump so you can't even watch us. That's your punishment for not cooperating," which was a word our teacher uses on our report cards. When we don't obey her or join the others in their play or work, she gives us a check mark in the square that says, "Does not cooperate." (That fall there was only one of the Sugar Creek Gang who had a check mark there, but I won't tell you which one of us it was because I don't think my parents would want anybody to know.)

Each one of our gang had his favorite swimming style. Little Jim used the breaststroke, which made him look like a white frog swimming in the water. Circus used the crawl stroke. In fact, most of us did. That's the kind of stroke many fast swimmers use. But Poetry, being an expert swimmer, had a newfangled stroke called the "trudgen." He just lay facedown in the water, rolled his barrel-like body from side to side, and swung his arms in long, overarm movements, each arm taking turns. His feet under the water worked like my mom's big silver-colored scissors do when they're cutting out a new dress for Charlotte Ann.

All the time I was in swimming I kept thinking about little brown-nosed Triangle up there on the bank behind the stump, and I thought, *What if the little fellow should slip the collar over his head and run away?* There was a big cornfield right there beyond the stump, and a baby bear might get lost in a cornfield, not having any mother to take care of him. And pretty soon it'd be fall and then winter. Or what if somebody who wanted to steal him and sell him to the zoo should sneak up and slip the collar off his neck and carry him away?

More than an hour later we sort of came to ourselves and realized we'd better get dressed to go home. Tomorrow would be Sunday, and we'd have to polish our shoes and do some extra chores on Saturday so we wouldn't have to do them Sunday. As I told you in my last book, all of our gang went to church and Sunday school. We felt sorry for any boy who didn't want to go and for all the kids whose parents didn't think a boy's soul was as important as the rest of him.

Imagine a boy going to school five days a week to learn reading, writing, arithmetic, geography, history, and other important things and then not go to church just once a week to learn about the Bible, which is the most important book in the world. It tells you how to be saved, which is even more important than being educated.

Well, Dragonfly got dressed first and ran up the bank toward the old stump to untie Triangle, with Little Jim and me right at his already-dirty bare heels. All of a sudden Dragonfly stopped dead in his tracks and cried, "Hey! He's *gone!* Triangle's *gone!* Somebody's stolen him!"

2

We couldn't believe our eyes, and yet we had to because Triangle *was* gone and only the chain and leather collar were there. Little Jim stood with the collar in his hand, looking down at the Bible verse on it with big tears in his eyes. Pretty soon a couple of his tears splashed out and fell on my bare toes because I was standing close to him.

I gulped and got mad instead of crying, because the leather collar had been cut in two with a knife. Somebody's boy hadn't been trained up in the way he ought to go. Whoever it was, I thought, it must have been somebody who didn't like us very well—that is, if he had just cut the collar so the bear could run away and hadn't stolen him.

Right away I thought of the Till boys, who lived on the other side of Sugar Creek. Their father was not a Christian, and they hadn't been to Sunday school and church in their lives. They belonged to a rough gang of boys that our gang had licked last summer in the Battle of Bumblebee Hill, the new name we gave that hill after the fight.

We were standing there and all talking at once with nobody listening to anybody when

Dragonfly, who had been looking around a little, yelled, "Hey! Come here, quick!"

And then we all saw what he saw: bear tracks going down a corn row, right behind a man's shoe prints, which were going in the same direction!

I never realized how much I liked the mischievous little rascal until right that minute. Of course, if the man—or whoever it was who had stolen him—would sell him to a zoo, he'd get plenty to eat, but he'd have to live in a cage all the time, I thought.

With Big Jim and Dragonfly in the lead, the rest of us followed, Little Jim carrying Triangle's chain and cut collar. We looked kind of like a funeral procession, I guess. Only we knew we weren't on our way to any graveyard unless it was to the baby bear's grave.

We kept on hurrying through the cornfield, behind Dragonfly and Big Jim, who were following Triangle's tracks. We were especially careful not to let the sharp edges of the sword-shaped corn blades cut our eyes.

All of a sudden we came out on the other side of the field, where there were a rail fence and a road. There the footprints disappeared, and we couldn't find them again. That meant, if my thoughts were right, that the man who had taken him and led him away had probably climbed into a truck or car and driven away with him.

Since we couldn't find any more tracks, Big Jim went back to study the ones we'd been following, which was hard to do because we'd all walked right along in them and most of them were covered up with barefeet tracks. Once Big Jim stooped down and looked a long time. Then he called us and said, "These tracks are a lot older than the bear's tracks. There are little dust spatters in them!"

Well, that settled that, and my great idea had been crazy, but just the same I hated to give it up. Of course, if I was wrong, it meant that Triangle had just run away and we'd probably find him, or our folks would, or somebody.

It wasn't far from where we were to the swamp and the old sycamore tree, where so many important things had happened, so we went there to talk things over and to decide what to do. Big Jim called a meeting, and it was while we were sitting there in the grass with a lot of gray-headed dandelions around, looking like old men who didn't have much longer to live, that I got to thinking about Old Man Paddler, who lived up in the hills.

He had taught us boys so many important things and had shown Little Jim how to teach Triangle to dance a jig. Old Man Paddler had had a pet bear cub himself once when he was a little boy almost seventy-five years ago. That bad little black, brown-nosed bear had liked Old Man Paddler almost as well as he had Little Jim.

Old Man Paddler wore long white whiskers and was the kindest man you ever saw, and he was happy. I heard my dad say once that the devil doesn't have any happy old men, which means that if you want to be happy when you're old, you'll have to start being a Christian when you're young.

That kind old man knew all about bears and pretty nearly everything else. You could ask him almost anything, and he could answer you. My dad said he had been a lawyer once. He had had three children, all of them boys, but none of them had lived to be more than twelve years of age. Then his wife died too and left him all alone in the world, and he had built a cabin up in the hills and lived alone. And after that, he'd rather do something for boys than anything else in the world, on account of not having any.

Well, while we were sitting under the old sycamore tree talking about what had happened to Little Jim's bear, I kept on thinking about Old Man Paddler, who had been a lawyer once, and I thought we might ask him what to do about getting the bear back.

Dragonfly thought we ought to tell the police—so that in case he had been stolen instead of having run away, they'd put detectives on the case.

Poetry didn't like that idea at all. He said the Sugar Creek Gang were better detectives than any policeman detectives, meaning he thought Poetry himself was pretty good.

"Didn't we catch that bank robber without any help?" Poetry asked, which was true. "And didn't we find Old Man Paddler and save his life? And didn't we kill a bear all by ourselves?" he finished.

Just then Circus rolled over and turned a somersault backward and said excitedly, "I'll go and get my dad's big hounds," meaning his father's long-eared, long-tongued, sad-faced hunting dogs. "And if we let 'em smell Triangle's collar," he explained, almost yelling, "they'll follow his tracks with their noses and find where he went."

That looked like the best thing to do, so we voted on it like grown-ups do in their business meetings. Poetry made what is called a "motion," saying, "I move we get Circus's hounds and let them trail Triangle."

Dragonfly said, "I second the motion," meaning, "I'm in favor of that too."

Then Big Jim said in a very businesslike voice, "It has been moved and seconded that we get Circus's hounds and that we let them trail Triangle. Are you ready for the question?" That meant he wanted to know if we were ready for him to ask how many of us wanted Circus to get his dad's dogs.

So I piped up and said, "Question."

Big Jim cleared his throat and said, "All in favor of the motion raise your right hand."

In a jiffy all our kind of dirty right hands were up in the air except Little Jim's, and it wasn't on account of his not knowing how to vote either. I looked at his eyes because I saw him give his head a toss the way he always does when he wants to get tears out of his eyes without letting anybody know there were any there.

Then Big Jim said, "Those opposed use the

same sign." And Little Jim's hand shot up as though he was waving good-bye to somebody he liked very much and wouldn't ever see again.

"The motion is carried," Big Jim said, which meant that most of us wanted the dogs, and the meeting was over. Pretty soon they'd put their noses on the collar and on Triangle's tracks and sniff. Then they'd go bawling and howling on the trail, following the tracks. Their noses can smell fresh animal tracks better than a hungry boy can smell fried potatoes at supper time.

Little Jim was too brave to cry, but his voice sounded as if it had tears in it when he said, stuttering a little, "Th-they'll c-catch T-Triangle and b-bite him and m-m-maybe t-t-t-tear him to pieces with their big sharp teeth!"

So, without calling another meeting, we decided right away, for Little Jim's sake, not to get the hounds.

Something had to be done, though. You can't let a baby bear run loose in a neighborhood—for he is bound to get into trouble. And maybe somebody who doesn't know he's a pet will see him and shoot him, or maybe somebody's dogs will kill him.

We finally decided to keep our eyes open and to go home and tell our folks he was lost and have them keep their eyes open for him too. We all felt sorry for Little Jim as well as for ourselves, because we all liked that "frowzy little fellow with a tail that isn't there." When anything is lost, you seem to like it even better.

Do you know what Little Jim said to me that

afternoon when he left our house to go on home? He was always piping up and saying something important. He said, "I'll bet that's why Jesus likes boys so well—'cause so many of them are lost. I'll bet He likes Tom Till an awful lot."

And that made me remember I'd promised my Sunday school teacher I'd go over and see little red-haired Tom Till and try to get him to come to Sunday school tomorrow, and I hadn't done it yet.

As I said, the very minute I knew Triangle was lost, I'd thought of the Till boys but especially of their mean-faced, hook-nosed father, who drank a lot and whose words most of the time were as filthy as a mud puddle in a barnyard. I don't know why I thought of him, but I did, and I felt sorry that Little Tom Till had to have that kind of a daddy. I was afraid of Big John Till too.

Well, a promise was a promise, so I decided I'd go over to Tom Till's house after supper and, while I was there, look around a little to see if I could find a brown-nosed bear cub with a white triangle on his breast. I wondered what would happen if I did find him. Or if John Till would get terribly mad at me for asking Tom to go to church with us tomorrow . . .

As soon as supper was over, I told Mom what I'd promised my teacher. Then I went in and looked at Charlotte Ann, who was asleep in her little Scottie dog bassinet. I took a big breath of fresh air and tried to feel brave, and I said to sleeping Charlotte Ann, "Little sister, I'm going to war now. I may come back with a broken arm or a black eye or something, but duty calls me."

I was hoping something very important about Tom Till, so I ran upstairs to get my New Testament. While I was in my room, I shut the door for a minute and went down on both of my knees, which is what I do when I pray. My dad says it takes a brave man to get down on his knees and pray all by himself.

Anyway, my knees were just beginning to feel a little bit tired on the hard floor when all of a sudden the door burst open, and my dad came in.

"Oh, excuse me," he said. "I didn't know you were here. I thought you'd gone."

I looked up quick, and there were tears under his big eyebrows. Then without even looking at me, he gave me a great big hug and said, still not looking at me, "I'd rather have a praying boy than any other kind, Bill. I'm sorry I interrupted you." Then he turned and went out and shut the door, and I finished what I was doing.

When I went downstairs, Dad was in our front room standing beside Mom, looking down into Charlotte Ann's bassinet, and he and Mom were hugging each other, which I always liked to see them do.

Then with my heart as light as a feather I went outdoors and jumped on my bicycle and pedaled down the road and onto the Sugar Creek bridge toward Tom Till's house, wondering all the time if anything important was going to happen to me before I got back.

3

When I was halfway across the bridge, I stopped, stood my bicycle up against the railing on the east side, and looked at the long shadow the sun made of me on the water. I looked like a giant a hundred feet tall. I didn't feel like one, though. I remembered Big John Till.

Then I rode on across the bridge. I always liked to hear the planks shaking when I went across. Some of the floorboards were loose and made a rattling noise whenever anybody rode over them. Sometimes, when I was at home in bed, I'd wake up in the middle of the night, hearing somebody's car or a horse and wagon going across.

The nearer I got to Tom Till's house, the more nervous I felt inside, and I think my heart must have been acting like Circus turning somersaults.

The house that Tom Till lived in wasn't much of a house, but that wasn't his fault. Besides, it's the kind of people that live in a house that's important anyway.

Tom and Little Jim had been friends ever since Little Jim killed the ferocious old mother bear and maybe saved Tom's life. And even though Tom and I had given each other a black eye in that gang fight, and even though each one of us had red hair, we sort of liked each other anyway.

I stopped at their battered old gate, afraid to go in. I kept my eyes peeled for Triangle or John Till or Tom's big brother, Bob, who was bigger even than Big Jim and almost as good a fighter.

Just that minute I glimpsed a bright red head of hair peeping around from behind a walnut tree, and I knew it was Tom Till. He looked as if he hadn't had a haircut all summer.

"Hello," I said, and Tom called back, "Hello."

"Want to play catch?" I asked. I took a big orange out of my pocket and threw it to him. I hadn't intended to throw it so high, but that little fellow leaped up in the air and caught it with one hand, which meant he'd make a good player on our school ball team that fall.

Pretty soon we were lying in the grass behind the fence, talking about different things. All the time I was wanting to tell him why I'd come over to his house, but I was afraid to. I could feel my New Testament in my pocket, and I kept thinking about Little Jim's favorite verse, which was in the Old Testament in Proverbs 22:6. But I was thinking especially of the story of the boy in the Bible who gave his lunch to Jesus one day, and Jesus fed a whole crowd of people with it. I wanted to tell Tom Till that Jesus liked boys and had actually died on the cross to save them, but—well, I just couldn't for a minute.

After a while, though, I decided it was silly to be afraid, so I said, "I promised my Sunday school teacher I'd ask you to go to Sunday school with me tomorrow."

He had the orange all peeled and was dividing it in half with his dirty hands, the juice washing off some of the dirt. And then he handed me the cleanest half and said, "Maybe I *can* come. I'm going to get some new clothes in town tonight. Dad's made a lot of money this week, and he's going to get me a new suit and shoes and everything."

I was surprised because I didn't know his dad had been working. For about nine seconds I couldn't do anything but stare at him, wondering where John Till had got all the money. I wiped off some of the dirt from my piece of orange and ate it and thought about Triangle and wondered if maybe he was already in a zoo somewhere or maybe riding along in a car or truck.

Then I started telling Tom about the Bible boy's lunch, which was a couple of fish and five little buns, called loaves.

"Where'd the boy get the fish?" Tom wanted to know.

I'd never thought about that, so I said, "I don't know, but maybe he'd been fishing in Lake Galilee. They say fishing was awful good there. I'll bet the boys who lived close to the lake had a lot of fun fishing and swimming and things. I'll bet Jesus Himself went fishing when He was a boy."

"Was Jesus a boy once?" Tom asked, surprised.

"Sure," I said. "He was even a little baby once. But He was up in heaven first, where He'd been all the time and where He was when He made the world and all the stars and things. Then He came to our earth to be our Savior, but the people didn't want to be saved, so they treated Him mean and even crucified Him and—"

"What's *crucified* mean?" Tom asked. Imagine his not knowing that!

Well, I explained to him different things, the way my dad and mom and my Sunday school teacher and Little Jim had explained them to me. Little Jim could explain things in boys' language, which made them easier to understand.

Then Tom Till said, "My daddy doesn't believe in Jesus."

Just that minute I heard loud talking in their house, and it was Big Bob Till talking back to his mother and saying, "I won't do it! I *hate* wiping dishes! You never let me do anything I want to!"

I felt my temper starting to catch on fire. Then I heard their back screen door open and slam shut, and I saw Big Bob Till shuffle out and grab his long cane fishing pole and start off toward the creek, though I couldn't see him very well. I was angry because I thought how his mother must feel. I wanted to jump up and run after Big Bob Till and give him a good pounding.

But I didn't. Instead, I looked over at Little

Tom, and I said, without knowing I was going to, "Let's you and me go in and help your mother with the dishes," which we did.

I guess I never felt so polite in my life as I did while we were walking around in their kitchen, drying the dishes and putting them away. Every now and then, when Tom's sad-faced mother wasn't looking, I'd look at her out of the corner of my eye. She looked like just any ordinary mother, who could be awful happy if she had a chance.

I decided that if Bill Collins or anybody that looked like him ever talked mean to *his* mother or wouldn't help her when she wanted him to and was too lazy to work, I'd sock him. Lazy old Bill Collins! I tell you I was mad, even at myself!

And the next day in church, when our new minister said it was sin that caused all the heartaches in the world, I felt something inside of me just boil up like a teakettle full of water when it gets hot. I wanted to take a great big gospel sword and go running through the world and cut to pieces all the sin everywhere.

Well, when we were through helping Tom's mom, I remembered I still had some chores to do at home, so I said, "Don't forget that Sunday school starts at ten. Be at our house at a quarter till, and you can ride with us."

I climbed on my bicycle and pedaled for home as fast as I could.

4

At a quarter to ten the next morning, Tom Till came over to our house in his new clothes and shoes and with his hair cut, looking like an ordinary boy.

He sat right beside me in our Sunday school class, and I tell you it felt good to think I'd invited him to come.

It was a great Sunday school lesson too, all about a blind man getting his eyesight back again. All that Jesus had to do was reach out and touch his eyes. I thought how, in the battle of Bumblebee Hill, Tom had blackened my eye and how I'd hated him so much I couldn't see straight. And now I didn't hate him anymore, and I decided maybe Somebody'd touched my eyes and healed me too.

Little Jim sat on the other side of Tom Till, and, in spite of myself, every time I looked down and saw Tom's new shoes with their shining black leather, my mind went splashing and diving along on the mystery of the lost bear.

After church was over, when I got a chance, I told Little Jim why I thought maybe Tom Till's father had stolen Triangle.

And do you know what Little Jim did? He smiled with big tears in his eyes and said, "I'm awful sorry to lose Triangle, but I'd rather have

Tom Till have new clothes and shoes and go to Sunday school than to have a pet bear." Then he gave his head a quick toss and shook most of the tears out of his eyes. He dabbed the rest of them dry with his handkerchief and said, "Let's you and me have a secret." He made me promise I wouldn't tell anybody about what I thought I knew, and I kept my promise.

In fact, I'm glad I *didn't* tell anybody, because that same day after dinner I found out that Triangle hadn't been stolen at all—although it was a mean trick to cut his beautiful new collar and let the little cub loose. Whoever had done it, I thought again, must have been somebody who didn't like the Sugar Creek Gang very well.

As soon as dinner was over at our house, Dad and I washed and dried the dishes, which we always do on Sunday because it's like saying thank you to Mom for the especially nice dinner she cooked for us. Except that it takes a lot longer to do the dishes than to just say two little words.

Charlotte Ann was supposed to be taking her nap and wasn't—on account of being disgusted about something—so she was doing what all babies do when they feel that way. I didn't like to hear her cry, so I went out to our big swing and sat there waiting for Little Jim to come over to play.

Dad took a walk down to our orchard, where he had his very best hive of bees with a whole lot of honey in it, which he was going to sell before long and buy me some new clothes.

Pretty soon I heard him calling, "Bill! Come here, quick!"

I was swinging, but as soon as I could get out of the swing without jumping off—which is dangerous if you're swinging very high—I ran out into the orchard to where Dad was.

He was pointing to something under an apple tree, and he said with a big voice, "Look what your famous pet bear did to my best beehive while we were in church this morning!"

I looked, and there was his biggest and best beehive turned over on its side. The upper part of it had burst open, and maybe a thousand bees were swarming in every direction, madder than anything.

I knew bears liked honey very, very much, but Old Man Paddler had told us it wasn't good for them to eat too many sweets because bears are what are called "carnivorous" animals. That means their main food is flesh of some kind, and too much honey or syrup will make them sick, just the way too many green apples or grapes would do to a boy.

I was standing looking at that turned-over beehive—glad that Triangle was still alive but worrying a little as to what might happen to him if he got a stomachache—when Dad said, "Do you know how much honey there was in the upstairs part of that hive?"

I said, "No. How much?"

He said, "About twenty pounds! I know because I looked in yesterday. Your bear has eaten at least fifteen pounds of the honey that I was going to sell to help pay for your clothes, you know."

In my mind I could see Little Jim's frowsy, brown-nosed baby bear with his fat little sides bulging with maybe twenty pounds of honey. And with his nose all swollen where the bees had stung him, which bees do when you try to take their honey. And I felt very sorry for him. I knew he'd be sick and might even die if somebody didn't find him and take care of him.

That afternoon my dad and our new minister and Little Jim's dad and Circus's dad and some of the musicians from our church went to hold a meeting in a jail in the city where there were a lot of men and older boys who hadn't been trained up in the way they ought to go. And that's why Little Jim and his mom came over to our house—to wait until the jail meeting was over.

The reason Circus's dad had gone to the jail meeting was that he was going to give what is called a "testimony," so all the men and boys in the jail could know that even an alcoholic could be saved if he would repent of his sins and believe on the Lord Jesus Christ.

Well, pretty soon Little Jim and I were out in our orchard looking at the overturned beehive, without getting close enough for the bees to see us and think we were the ones that had broken up their home. Bees aren't able to see very well, and sometimes I don't believe they think at all.

All of a sudden I got to thinking that what I

wanted to do more than anything else right that minute was to find that little bear so we could nurse him back to health in case he was sick. I knew the quickest way to find him was to put Circus's dad's big dogs on his trail. I thought if Big Jim and Circus would hold the dogs back by strong leashes, we could follow right along behind them and find the bear, and the dogs wouldn't hurt him because we wouldn't let them. I knew I'd have to make Little Jim see how important it was, or he wouldn't let us do it.

I guess I was thinking about how much fun all that would be too. In fact, I was.

Well, I told Little Jim what my dad said had happened.

He looked at the broken beehive and said, "I wonder how much he ate."

I said, "Maybe ten or fifteen or even twenty pounds."

Little Jim stooped down to tie his shoestring, which had come untied. While he was still stooped over, he said with a grunt, "Do you suppose he got stung very bad?"

"Maybe a thousand times," I said. Then I remembered that bees can't sting through a bear's heavy fur. They *can* sting his nose and mouth though, unless he puts his paws up to protect himself. Even then, when he's eating honey he's bound to get stung pretty bad.

"He probably ate a thousand bees too," I said, "'cause the bees crawl over the honey all the time, and he might get a terrible stomachache."

Then Little Jim said, "Do you suppose the bees could sting him on the inside?"

"They might," I said. "Anyway, he'll probably need a doctor." Then I reminded him of what Old Man Paddler had said about bears being carnivorous and how they shouldn't eat too much honey or syrup or they'd have what is called "dietary" trouble.

I guess that long word scared Little Jim because the first three letters of it spell the word *die*. Anyway, when I mentioned the hounds and explained how we could hold them back from hurting that fat little Triangle, Little Jim changed his mind, and in less than two minutes we were on my bicycle pedaling down the road toward Circus's house.

He lived right across the road from Big Jim. And Poetry was already there, so that was all of us except Dragonfly, who couldn't have been with us anyway because his parents had gone to another town to visit a cousin of his.

We took two of those big dogs, Big Jim holding one leash and Circus the other, and away we went by a shortcut through the woods to my house. It certainly didn't take long for those dogs to find Triangle's trail. The very minute their long noses smelled it, they started acting crazy. We could hardly keep up with them, they went so fast, almost dragging Big Jim and Circus. Little Jim and Poetry and I followed along behind.

Away we went, out across our orchard and through a hole in the fence where there was some hair caught in the wires—maybe because Triangle's sides were so fat, I thought—across the road and straight for Sugar Creek, where all of a sudden the trail was lost.

The hounds, with their tails whirling as if they were trying to crank a couple of old-fashioned cars and with their noses close to the ground, whined and acted worried and ran up and down the creek bank.

"I'll bet Triangle jumped in the creek to get the bees off him," Poetry said.

And Little Jim said, "M-m-maybe he got drowned!"

But Circus said, "He'd be so fat with all that honey in him that he'd float—like Poetry."

And Poetry said, making up a poem:

"A little round bear
    with a little round tummy
That sank when he swam
    like a tub full of honey."

It was funny, but for some reason none of us laughed.

The dogs kept running up and down, dragging Circus and Big Jim after them. Then suddenly one of them let out a long, high-pitched bawl, which meant he'd found the trail again.

We all ran as fast as we could to where he'd found it, and there as plain as day was a bear's track—a whole lot of them, in fact, right there in the cool mud. I remembered from the books I'd read in Dad's library that bears actually plaster clay on their noses and faces when they get stung by bees, so it won't hurt so much and will get well quicker.

Right away we were running again, following the dogs along the bank of Sugar Creek, right past the old swimming hole and through the swamp, straight for the hills.

The dogs acted more and more excited all the time, as though the trail was getting what Circus called "hot," which meant we were about to catch up with the bear.

Little Jim puffed beside me. "I'll bet Triangle went up to Old Man Paddler's cabin."

I was thinking the same thing. We'd all been up there with him two or three times during the summer. In fact, the old man always fed Triangle a nice fat mouse he had caught in a trap the night before. There are mice around any cabin that is built in the woods, and every time we'd taken Triangle up there, Old Man Paddler had a mouse to give him.

When we were going through the swamp, the dogs lost their trail for a minute, and Little Jim happened to remember it was Sunday. He wondered if it would be all right for us to go hunting on Sunday, because our gang didn't do some things that other people did on Sundays.

But Poetry remembered a Bible verse that said it was all right to help a sheep get out of the ditch if it fell in on the Sabbath.

And Little Jim said, "Does it say anything about a bear being lost, and that it's all right to look for him with dogs?"

We decided that if it was all right to help get a sheep out of a ditch on the Sabbath, it would be all right to help save a little bear's life. So when the dogs found the trail again, we hurried right along after them.

Pretty soon the dogs were at the old man's cabin, their tails whirling and their voices sounding like a baby taking a walk across the keys of the organ at our church.

In a minute the door opened, and Old Man Paddler was standing in the doorway with his long white whiskers covering most of his chest. He took off his heavy glasses so he could see us better—he only used them when he wanted to see something up close, such as when he read or ate.

Circus made the dogs quit barking, and the old man said, "Well, well, where's Dragonfly?" He knew us all by name, and he even called us by our nicknames, which made us know he liked us. And it helped us to like him even better.

"Dragonfly went to visit his cousin," Poetry said.

Then the old man threw back his fine old white head and laughed and said, "It seems like a good day for visitors. If you boys will tie up your dogs and come in, I'll let you see my company, but be very quiet because this cabin is a hospital now."

Pretty soon we were all in the main room of the cabin. It took a minute for our eyes to get adjusted so we could see clearly. I looked around, and there was the cookstove, a table, three or four chairs, a nice clean cot over in the corner, and a high stack of wood along the wall, which my dad and some other men had cut last summer and which the Sugar Creek Gang had carried into the cabin ourselves so there'd be plenty of firewood for the next winter.

Then I saw the big stone fireplace, and there, right in the middle of it, was Triangle, lying very quiet and breathing hard as if he was sick. Sure enough, he had gone to Old Man Paddler's cabin. Maybe he knew that, with all the honey in him, he'd need some meat quick so he wouldn't get too sick, and he had thought of how good a nice fat mouse would taste. There was clay packed on his nose and face, and his fat little sides were sticking out as though he had eaten even more than twenty pounds of honey.

Little Jim was so happy he almost screamed, and he started toward the fireplace to hug Triangle, he was so glad to see him again.

But the old man stopped him. "He's very cross now, because he is sick, but he'll get well in a few days, and then you may play with him again. I'll nurse him back to health as soon as I can. I'll give him plenty of medicine, but I think you'd better leave him right here with me until he is well."

"What kind of medicine?" Little Jim wanted to know.

"Nature's medicine," the old man said. "Just good sweet milk and plenty of fresh meat, and *no* honey or syrup or candy. Maybe you boys can arrange with your folks to bring up milk and meat every day for a while."

So that was the way we got Little Jim's bear back, and we were all happy again.

5

Winter was getting ready to come out of the north to visit us. School was in full swing, and we were all busy with lessons and tests and hard study, and of course a lot of good hard play too. Nothing very important happened for a while until Big Jim and Big Bob Till got into a fierce fight in which Big Jim almost got licked, and maybe would have if—but let me tell you about it.

It happened on the way home from school one afternoon, and it was all on account of Big Bob Till saying some rough words to a new girl who had moved into our neighborhood. As I told you, we had a new minister in our church, and she was his daughter and was almost as good a Christian as Little Jim. And she wasn't stuck-up, the way some girls are.

Like most boys, none of our gang played with girls much, although we knew they belonged to the human race. And I realized we ought to be kind to them. My mom had been a girl once herself, and if my mom had been one, then girls must be all right.

The new girl was named Sylvia, and she was in the eighth grade and was very smart. She had curly brown hair that hung down the back of her neck.

I could see right away that Big Jim thought Sylvia was pretty nice, because after she started coming to our school I noticed he combed his hair a little straighter. And when we played prisoner's base, he tried especially hard not to let her be a prisoner very long.

Big Bob Till must have noticed Big Jim being extra courteous to Sylvia, and he didn't like it. He must have had an awful dirty mind, for half the time his words were even worse than his father's were. He was always telling bad things about girls, which filthy-minded boys and men sometimes do.

None of our gang ever talked like that, not only because Big Jim wouldn't stand for it but because we had sense enough not to. We wouldn't let anybody else do it when they were with us either. In fact, I had a hard time to keep from punching any boy in the nose whenever I heard him using dirty words. As I may have told you once before, all our gang were Christians, and we weren't ashamed of it, and we felt sorry for any boy who was afraid to be one for fear some ignorant person would make fun of him.

It's silly to be afraid to be a Christian. If they still burned people alive because they are Christians—the way they used to hundreds of years ago— and if they decided to burn up the Sugar Creek Gang, I'll bet Little Jim would stand there looking at the great big yellow flames, and, even though he might be scared almost to death, he'd start to sing one of his favorite songs:

"Dare to be a Daniel, dare to stand alone,
Dare to have a purpose true,
Dare to make it known."

Then if he had to, for Jesus' sake, he'd say,
"All right! Put me into that old fire, if you want
to! I won't deny Jesus!"

Well, when school was out that afternoon,
all seventeen students came scrambling out the
only door the little red brick schoolhouse had
and started home. They scattered like the bird-
shot out of my dad's shotgun—or maybe like
honeybees crawling out of a hive and then flying away.

Now, our teacher had a rule that there wasn't
to be any fighting on the way home from school
and that all boys had to be courteous to girls.

Sylvia and her little sister, Jeanelle, who was
in the third grade, had to walk home on the
same road our gang did. They lived farther away
from school than any of the rest of us—about a
mile up the road from my house. And there
weren't any school buses, so sometimes their
parents would come and get them in their car,
especially if it was a rainy day.

Our gang always walked home together as
far as we could, wrestling and balancing on top
of the rail fences and acting like frisky young
colts after they had been shut up in a barn all
day. Sometimes we'd take a shortcut through
the woods so we could be together a little
longer. Big Jim and Circus would walk almost
all the way home with Poetry and me. We'd all

go down Poetry's lane, and then they'd climb the fence and go through the woods and get home just as quick.

I noticed that Big Jim had been walking with Poetry and me nearly every night since Sylvia started coming to our school. Of course, we didn't all walk in one bunch like geese or ducks when they're going someplace but were all strung out, boys walking with boys and girls with girls.

That afternoon we were walking along, Poetry and Big Jim and all the gang and Sylvia and Jeanelle and Circus's kind of ordinary-looking sister—the one I was going to kill a spider for if I got a chance. It wasn't because I *liked* Circus's sister the way I thought Big Jim did Sylvia, but because there was something inside of me that made me want to be kind to some girl. Her name was Lucille, which wasn't a bad name.

While I was walking along beside Poetry and Big Jim, carrying my lunch bucket, I kept wishing that I could start running as fast as I could and turn a handspring in the grass the way Circus was doing right that minute, but I knew I'd make a fizzle of it and maybe get my nose bumped.

Then I got to thinking. What if some boy would run real fast and grab Lucille's hair ribbon and throw it away? I could run and pick it up and give it back to her, so she'd smile back at me when I grinned at her across the schoolroom when I wasn't supposed to.

While I was thinking that, all of a sudden

Big Bob Till, who had had to stay in after school because he'd done or said something he shouldn't have, came running down the road, leaping and yelling. He whizzed right past us boys and made a beeline for Sylvia. Before I could even guess what he was going to do, he snatched away her lunch box and threw it over the fence, where it landed out in the cornfield.

Then he called out to her roughly, "Old smarty! There goes your lunch box and all your brains with it! I wouldn't have had to stay in after school if you hadn't told on me!"

In a dignified voice, Sylvia said, "I didn't tell Miss Mulder anything, although someone should have. Such language! A gentleman wouldn't say such things as you said to me today!"

Sylvia had a low voice that sounded as if her mother had given her good training. Last Sunday she sang a solo in church, and it had sounded very pretty. The words were:

What a wonderful, wonderful Savior,
Who would die on the cross for me!

Then her father, our new minister, had preached a sermon about the man Lazarus being raised from the dead. Lazarus was buried in a cave, and there was a big stone rolled against the mouth of the cave. Some of Jesus' friends rolled the rock away, and, just as soon as Jesus called and told Lazarus to come out, all of a sudden there he was, alive and well. Just think of it! And he'd been dead for four days! He was still wrapped up in grave clothes, and Jesus said, "Unbind him, and let him go."

Well, I thought Sylvia was right. Certainly no gentleman would say and do what Big Bob Till had said and done.

I guess Big Jim was thinking the same thing, only his thoughts must have been boiling hot. When he saw that lunch box sail over the fence into the cornfield, he stopped dead still. His jaw clicked shut, and his fists doubled up, and I knew from the way I'd felt at different times in my life that something was going to happen.

Just then Big Bob Till said something to Sylvia even worse than he had said to her on the school ground. And the next thing I knew I was holding Big Jim's lunch box in one hand and mine in the other, and Big Jim was shooting like an arrow straight for that big foul-mouthed bully.

Big Bob Till must have been expecting something like that. I suppose he hadn't forgotten the way Big Jim had licked the daylights out of him last summer on Bumblebee Hill, and maybe he'd been planning to get revenge. He knew a lot of wrestling tricks too. He whirled around and stooped low just as Big Jim got there. He grabbed Big Jim around the knees, turned a backward somersault, and threw him clear over his head.

Big Jim landed with a thud flat on his back in the grass. And before you could say Gingerbernooster, Bob was on top of him, slamming him with his fists and yelling, "You fuzzy-mustached, churchgoing sissy! You're going to get—" Then Bob swore, using the same words his father does when *he* swears.

Little Jim beside me was as white as a sheet. Little Jeanelle was crying. Lucille looked scared. And Sylvia stood looking kind of like a queen who had lost her crown.

I stood watching, with the two lunch boxes in my hands. I kept wondering why Big Jim didn't turn over and shove that bully off him and fight the way I knew he could. Then I noticed that he had turned pale as though he was sick. Then I heard him groan, and I knew he was already beaten. If somebody didn't help him, maybe Bob's hard fists would break his nose.

It didn't take me long to get rid of those lunch boxes. I didn't even take time to see where they fell. I made a flying tackle for one of Bob's legs, got hold of it, shut my eyes, and held on for dear life. I started pulling and yanking and twisting. Whenever I heard Big Jim groan, I felt myself getting madder, because I could still hear Bob's fists whamming away at him.

And then Poetry and Circus were in the fight, and somebody else too. A little later, when we got ourselves untangled, what do you suppose we found out? At first I couldn't believe my eyes, but the reason we could finally pull Bob Till off Big Jim was not only because Poetry and Circus had helped but because Little Tom had gotten hold of his brother's other leg and was fighting on our side!

Now we had Bob down on his stomach with Poetry sprawled across his shoulders, and the rest of us holding his arms and legs. On the ground beside us was Big Jim, with Little Jim and Dragonfly trying to help him sit up. You see, when Big Jim landed on his back, there'd been a rock in the grass that had hurt his back so much he hadn't been able to fight at all.

In a minute Little Tom Till got up and climbed over the fence and got Sylvia's lunch box. He came back and handed it to her bashful-like, without looking up, so he didn't see her smile.

But we all heard her say, "Thank you, Tom. You're a gentleman."

And I wished I'd been Tom myself. From that minute on, I knew Tom and I were going to be good friends, and maybe he'd even belong to the Sugar Creek Gang someday.

6

We didn't dare let Bob Till up, because he was still angry and might do something desperate, so we kept on holding him down. It was especially easy because there were so many of us.

But it was hard for Poetry to stay angry very long. Nearly everything anybody said or did reminded him of a poem. So while he was still holding Bob's shoulders down, he lifted his head and saw all of us with our arms and legs tangled up. It must have made him think of a centipede, which is a many-legged insect, so he began to quote:

"A centipede was happy quite
    Until a frog, in fun,
Said, 'Pray, which leg comes after which?'
    This roused his mind to such a pitch,
He lay distracted in the ditch,
    Considering how to run."

Bob Till, lying there in the ditch, did have a lot of legs on him, only they were boys' legs, and they weren't all his own. He had Poetry's, mine, and Circus's, plus his own, which is eight, and if you counted each arm for a leg, that'd make sixteen.

Well, we had to do something with our centipede, so we decided to ask Big Jim.

Big Jim still looked pale. He struggled to his feet and stood looking down at us as though he thought we were worth a million dollars. Then he turned to Sylvia and said, "He's your prisoner, Sylvia. What shall we do with him?"

I don't know what I expected her to say, but I thought he ought to have *some* kind of punishment, such as being thrown into Sugar Creek with his clothes on.

Sylvia looked like a queen again. I felt proud that Big Jim liked her. She not only got good grades in school, but if the church gave grades for the ones that were the best Christians, she would have had an "A" in everything. *Someday we might even decide to let her belong to our gang,* I thought. Big Jim could be the king and she the queen.

Sylvia stood there in the road with the September wind blowing some of her hair across her forehead, and she said—and I guess she must have heard her dad say it first—"Bob doesn't need to be punished. He needs to be changed." Her voice was so kind it sounded as if she was sorry for him.

Bob squirmed and begged us to let him up so he could breathe, so we made Poetry get off his shoulders, but we wouldn't let him up yet.

Do you know what Sylvia decided to do with Bob? I guess she knew that his dad was not a Christian and that Bob had never been to church in his life, so she decided that now would be as good a time as any for him to hear his first sermon.

When Little Jim saw what was going to happen, his eyes got all shiny. Circus's monkey face looked kind of like Sugar Creek's face does when there isn't any wind. Big Jim's eyes were looking at Sylvia.

She started talking, and that was the grandest "church service" I ever went to in my life, even if it did last only seven or eight minutes. We didn't have any piano or organ or hymnbooks or choir, and nobody said "Amen" out loud. But I kept thinking all the time, "Attagirl, Sylvia!" which is about the same as "Amen," only it isn't quite as reverent, and people don't say it in church. But I'll bet Jesus knew what I was thinking and was glad.

We had flowers though, as churches generally have. All along the rail fence were beautiful goldenrod that nodded their heads in the wind every now and then as if they were saying the same thing I was thinking.

And if you take a look at a goldenrod up close, it looks like the chandelier that hangs from the ceiling in the middle of our church, with maybe eight or ten different lights fastened to one stem. Only the goldenrod doesn't hang down but holds its head up toward the sky, as Sylvia's dad says Christians can do when their sins are all forgiven.

While she was talking, a flock of noisy blackbirds flew over the cornfield and started holding a convention in the old hickory tree across the road. They made me think again of the black notes on Little Jim's music sheets—so we had music even if it was out of tune.

Pretty soon the blackbirds got so noisy that we couldn't hear Sylvia very well. And that broke up our meeting, but not till Bob had heard enough to know that he was lost and could be saved—if he wanted to be and would repent of his sins and believe that Jesus Christ had come out of the grave after dying for all our sins and was alive now and would come into any boy's heart if he wanted Him to.

When Sylvia finished telling Bob what everybody in the world ought to know, she said to us, "Unbind him, and let him go," which we did.

The minute Big Bob was free, he looked around as if he couldn't see very well, and I thought I saw a tear trying to get out of one of his eyes, a little like the moon trying to get out from behind a big black cloud. And then he was on his feet and over the fence and running toward home without saying a word.

I guess maybe he was pretty surprised that we didn't give him some hard punishment. I also decided maybe he was in a hurry to get away, so that in case the tear got bigger and fell out of his eye, it would fall where nobody could see it.

When I got home that afternoon a little later than usual, I set my lunch box on our kitchen table, ate the sandwich Mom had left for me, and went out to gather the eggs, which was one of my chores and a lot of fun.

One of our old white hens always laid her egg in a nest in the haymow, so I had to climb up there each day to get it, that is, unless she didn't happen to lay an egg that day. Sometimes hens don't.

When I was up there that afternoon, I got to thinking about the time I'd tucked my little New Testament in a crack away up in a corner and decided to leave it until Circus's father would get saved. I'd gone up there every day and read it because that was one of my rules—to read the Bible every day.

Well, I thought, if Circus's dad could be saved, then why not Big Bob Till? I stood there on a pile of alfalfa hay, which cows like so well, and I listened. Nobody seemed to be downstairs. At least not any people. I did hear old Mixy, our black-and-white cat, mewing as if she was lonesome. I took my New Testament out of my pocket and read a very interesting chapter.

The Bible has some places that even grown-ups can't understand without studying them. My dad has a lot of different books that help to explain these places, which is what all boys' parents should have so they can answer all the hard questions that come popping into a boy's head —and just as quick come tumbling out of his mouth.

I finished reading my chapter. Then I climbed over the hay to the place where the crack was in the log, and there was a spiderweb right across the crack. Then I put both knees down on the hay and prayed for Bob Till, even if I didn't like him very well. *Then* I left the New Testament and climbed down and went on gathering eggs.

Pretty soon I came to the ladder that leads up, higher and higher, all the way up to the cupola —the tiny room on the tip-top of our barn. I always liked to climb up there and look out the glass windows across the cornfields and up along Sugar Creek. There were a lot of spiderwebs up there too, so I couldn't help but remember that I'd planned to kill a spider for Lucille Browne, Circus's kind of ordinary-looking sister. In fact, she was more than kind of ordinary-looking. Anyway, I decided if I was to kill a spider for her, I'd better hurry up and do it, or pretty soon it'd be winter and there wouldn't be any spiders to kill.

After supper, while the sun was still up pretty high, Little Jim's mom sent him over to our house on an errand and told him he could stay a while and play. Then, just before dark, I could ride him home on the back of my bicycle. I asked Dad if we could go down to the spring and get a drink, and he said we could but not to go in swimming, which we didn't want to do anyway.

Pretty soon away we went as fast as we could run, Little Jim running like a little cottontail and I like a big long-legged jackrabbit. I guess I'd grown about two inches that summer and was beginning to be all hands and feet, which made me look more and more like Bill Collins, which wasn't much. But Little Jim liked me and didn't care how I looked on the outside.

Each of us took a drink of water at the spring, lying down on our stomachs and trying to drink like birds do. They dip their bills in the water, you know, and scoop up a billful and then tip their heads up so the water'll run down their throats. They keep their bills moving all the time their heads are up, as though they are saying and thinking something cheerful.

Little Jim was lying on the other side of the spring from me. We could see the reflections of our heads in the pool of water, which looked almost like a mirror. All of a sudden he said, "Do you know what the birds say when they tip their heads up like that when they're drinking?"

I said, "No. What?"

And he said, "They say, 'Thank You, heavenly Father.'"

Little Jim was always surprising people by saying wise things like that. You never could tell what important thoughts might be hiding just behind those two blue eyes of his.

I didn't say anything, but I liked Little Jim better than ever.

Soon we had our shoes and socks off, which our parents hadn't said we couldn't do, and waded down along the creek, skipping rocks and making old Sugar Creek's face smile or frown, whichever we wanted. We'd throw in two stones at once, one a little farther out than the other, to make eyes; then one in the middle for a nose; then we'd skip another stone, making a long water furrow all the way across for a mouth.

When we were tired of doing that, we decided to walk past the old swimming hole just to remember the good times we'd had there and to feel sad because the summer was gone. When we got there we stopped a minute, and all of a sudden we heard somebody coming.

We ducked down behind a bed of wild irises, whose flowers had bloomed last summer from May to July. Dad says the iris gets its name from the Greek word meaning "rainbow," and its flowers do look a little like rainbows, except there is too much blue. My mom has some all-white and all-yellow irises in our garden.

Little Jim and I stayed as quiet as we could, and I kept my eyes wide open, looking between two long, sword-shaped leaves to see who was coming. I couldn't help but think about the time Little Jim's bear had run away, and I wondered again who had cut his collar and turned him loose. In fact, right that minute we were lying in the very spot where Triangle had been tied.

Also right that minute I was feeling something hard in the grass under my elbow. While we were keeping quiet, waiting to see who was coming, I looked to see what the hard thing was, and I almost hollered, I was so surprised. For right in front of my astonished eyes and by my shaky right hand was a big jackknife with the blade open. It was rusty, as if it had been lying there all summer in the sun and rain!

I didn't have time to think because at that second whoever was coming stopped on the other side of the willow shrub from us and began looking around as if he was trying to find something.

Little Jim nudged me, and my heart started beating fast because it was Circus himself! I thought something I shouldn't have thought and couldn't help thinking. I thought, *What if it was Circus who had cut the little bear loose and had lost his knife there and was looking for it now?* But that idea was silly because Circus had been in swimming with us at the time.

Or what if it had been Circus's dad, who used to do bad things before he was saved? What if that day last summer he had planned to steal Triangle and sell him and then had heard us coming and had to get away quick? But I didn't like to think that either. When a man gets saved, he doesn't steal anymore, does he?

We couldn't do anything but lie still and wait, not being able to see very well now because Circus was on the other side of the big shrub. Pretty soon he took off his old straw hat and shinnied up a little elm tree. I never saw a boy who could climb a tree so fast.

The next thing I knew, he was standing on a limb with his back to us, and what do you think he did up there? I couldn't believe my ears at first, but I had to. Circus began to sing. *Sing!* And the song he was singing was one of the songs in our hymnbook at church.

I looked at Little Jim, and he looked at me, and his eyes were shining as if he was very proud of Circus. It was the first time I'd heard

Circus sing by himself. He usually sang with some of our gang sitting beside him in church —with maybe Poetry's squawky voice growling along beside him and keeping anybody from hearing how good Circus's voice really was. *His voice is almost as pretty as a meadowlark's,* I thought, which is as clear as a flute.

Well, Circus stood up there in that swaying elm sapling, singing and maybe imagining he was standing before a big crowd. His high soprano quavered out across the creek like an owl's voice does at night.

The song he was singing was Dragonfly's favorite, and I wished he'd been there to hear it. I'll write down only the first verse for you, because I suppose nearly every boy or girl who goes to Sunday school or church knows it. It starts like this:

> I will sing the wondrous story,
> Of the Christ who died for me,
> How He left His home in glory,
> For the cross of Calvary.

Little Jim reached his little brown hand over to me and nudged me and whispered, "It's going to be a surprise for church tomorrow morning. My mother is teaching Circus to sing it." Little Jim's mother was a wonderful musician and our church pianist.

I guess Sylvia's father had found out right away that Circus had a good voice, so he decided to put it to work. That's because anybody that has a good voice ought to use it and not let it get rusty like an old knife that's been lost.

Well, I had that rusty-bladed knife in my pocket right that minute, and I was wondering whose it was, even while I was listening to Circus sing.

Then Little Jim and I began to feel that we'd better go away. Circus was just practicing, and he wouldn't want anybody to listen to him, so we sneaked away through the bushes and the tall weeds.

Later, while we were walking along, I got to thinking about a story in my Bible storybook about a man named Moses. He saw a bush on fire, which wasn't burning up because God Himself was right in the middle of it. God's big, kind voice called to Moses and said for him to take off his shoes because the ground he was standing on was holy ground. It was holy because God was there. I'll bet I felt the way Moses did.

My dad says there isn't any scientist in the world who can explain why the sun doesn't burn up. There is something in it that makes it keep on just as it is, all the time, like the burning bush in the Bible story. And if there wasn't any sun, we'd all freeze to death quick, so it's silly to be like John Till, who couldn't live a minute by himself if it wasn't for God keeping him alive.

Anyway, there was more than one surprise for the people in our church the next Sunday morning.

I guess Sylvia's dad knew and liked boys even better than our other minister had. He must have thought boys were important, because he made us feel that he needed us. Just before Circus sang his solo, Mr. Johnson, that being our minister's last name, gave a fine talk about boys, saying that all the great men in the world had had to be boys first, whether they wanted to or not. Then he asked Little Jim to come up to the platform and tell us a short story, just as teachers do in school, and this is what Little Jim said:

"Once upon a time there was a man named Peter Bilhorn, who made his living playing the piano in a saloon for the men who bought and drank their whiskey there. One night while Peter was sitting at the piano in the smoky room, some Christian workers came in and gave him a piece of paper called a tract that had the gospel printed on it. Peter got mad and tore it up. They gave him another tract, and he was still madder. He tore that one up too. Then they gave him another, and he folded it and put it in his pocket, because he had had a good Christian mother who wanted him to be saved and who had prayed for him. Then Peter went to a special meeting and let Jesus come into his heart, and after that he became a famous songwriter, and he wrote the song called 'I Will Sing the Wondrous Story.'"

When Little Jim finished his true story, he stood there a moment like a chipmunk standing on a stump along Sugar Creek just before it makes a dive for the ground and goes whisking away somewhere. Then Little Jim, with his blue eyes looking as innocent as Charlotte Ann's, came back to our row, squeezed his way past my mom and my dad, and sat down beside me. He was trembling like a scared baby rabbit in a boy's hand, but he looked happy.

In a half minute we were all listening to Circus sing Peter Bilhorn's song while Little Jim's mom, who had on a new fall hat that looked like a small sunflower upside down, played the piano for him.

Little Tom Till was sitting on the other side of me, with one eye swollen a little bit as if he'd been in another fight. It made me feel all clean inside when I thought about how I'd invited him to come to church the first time, and he actually seemed to like to come.

After church and just before we went home, we were out under a big locust tree on our church lawn. I asked Tom where he got his black eye, knowing I hadn't done it this time.

At first he didn't want to tell me. Then he looked around to be sure nobody else could hear, and he said, "Bob gave it to me for fighting on your side after school Friday."

And I knew the Sugar Creek Gang was going to have still more trouble with the oldest Till boy.

Just then I happened to think about the knife I'd found, so I took it out of my pocket and was starting to scrape one of my fingernails when Little Tom said, surprised, "Where'd you get that knife?"

I said, "Oh, nowhere. I just found it!"

"Let me see it," he said, just as Poetry came over to where we were.

Tom held the knife a while, turning it over and over, and looking strange. Then he said, "See that little nick in the handle?"

I said, "Yes."

And he said, "I'll bet it's the knife Bob lost. His had a nick in the same place."

That made it look more than ever as if Bob Till had been the one who'd cut Triangle's collar that day.

7

Fall was coming fast, and all the birds that had gotten married in the spring and their little baby birds that had grown up began to gather in flocks, the way boys do in gangs, only some of them weren't so noisy, and they didn't turn somersaults or walk on their hands.

Blackbirds gathered in one flock, sparrows in another, and crows in another. As soon as the leaves began to fall, about a thousand crows gathered in our woods, and I never heard such noise as when their hoarse voices cawed all day long. They flew around from one place to another and back again and up and down from the trees to the ground, scolding all the time.

There had been a family of swallows in our garage, having made their nest up on a beam. You know that a pair of swallows sometimes have two or three broods of baby birds in one summer in the same nest. Ours had quadruplets the first time, quintuplets the second, and sextuplets the third, making fifteen new swallow children in one summer! But when fall started to come, they were all gone. I suppose they'd joined a lot of others that were flying up and down Sugar Creek just above the water, up and down, crossing and crisscrossing, their tails shaped like the fork of a boy's slingshot.

I knew that Jack Frost would come soon and kill all our garden stuff, and after that old Grandpa Winter himself would come with his snow-white whiskers, and it'd be terribly cold.

And that reminded me of Old Man Paddler, whose life our gang saved once and who told us that someday when he died there'd be something for each one of us in his will. And that reminds me that pretty soon, just as soon as I get to it, I'd better keep the promise I made in my story *The Killer Bear* and tell you what happened that winter on a cold—*very* cold —day when our gang went up to see the old man.

Fall comes before winter though. In the fall, Jack Frost paints all the leaves in the woods yellow, gold, and red, besides killing all the flowers and garden things. Pretty soon there wouldn't be any butterflies or caterpillars or spiders. And I got to thinking it was time I killed that spider I'd planned to.

At last one day I got a chance, although I hadn't planned on nearly everybody in our school being present when it happened, and I certainly hate to tell you what *did* happen, but I suppose you'll want to know—or do you?

The idea first came to me back in the middle of the summer when Little Jim picked up a baby bird that had fallen out of its nest and very carefully put it back. He wrapped his handkerchief around it first so the mother bird wouldn't smell where his hand had touched her baby and maybe kill it, as some mother birds do when a boy's hands have handled their babies. That's why a boy ought not to take a baby bird out of its nest and play with it.

When that fuzzy, scrawny, bulging-eyed, big-mouthed cute baby bird was in its nest again beside its brothers and sisters, Little Jim and I watched them a few minutes while the mother bird and her husband and all the neighbor birds scolded in the trees and bushes around us. Then we went away.

And I thought of Charlotte Ann, who was even more helpless than a baby bird, and I thought I ought to be very kind to her. Then I thought that a boy should be kind to *all* girls. They are such helpless things and are afraid of mice and spiders and worms and june bugs and caterpillars and centipedes.

So when school started and I saw that Big Jim was especially kind to Sylvia, I knew it'd be all right for me to be especially courteous to Circus's kind of ordinary-looking sister, Lucille —who, when she was wearing a blue hair ribbon, didn't look so ordinary—even though she didn't exactly act as helpless as a baby bird, and I'd never heard her scream when she saw an ugly caterpillar crawling toward her.

At school one day we were sitting out behind the woodshed at noon, eating our lunch. Sylvia and another girl and Lucille were on one end of a long log, and Poetry and Dragonfly and I were sitting on the other end, with about three feet between Lucille and me.

I had three apples in my lunch box. All of a

sudden I thought of the baby bird Little Jim had put back in the nest, and how helpless it was, and how mother birds bring worms and caterpillars and things and feed their bird babies. That made me think of how girls are afraid of caterpillars and spiders. So when nobody was looking, I slipped my reddest, shiniest apple over into Lucille's lunch box.

She smiled just the way Charlotte Ann does when Mom gives her a bite of spinach, which she likes very much. Then her face turned redder than our old red rooster's comb had been before he got killed.

I kept on eating and was talking to Poetry when all of a sudden Big Bob Till came walking past, swinging a baseball bat. He stopped and looked at Dragonfly and Poetry and me and said to us, "Will you girls hurry up and get through eating so we can play ball?"

It didn't take me even a tenth of a minute to get angry at being called a girl, so I shouted at Big Bob Till to go and tend to his own business. With Lucille sitting beside me, not more than three feet away, I even felt big enough to give Big Bob a licking.

"My business," Bob Till said sarcastically, "is to upset the log you're sitting on!" And with that remark he shoved his baseball bat under the log and gave a mighty heave.

Over went the log and three boys and three girls and six lunch boxes, each one going in a different direction.

Then, out from under the log scrambled a

64

big, long-legged brown spider that started straight toward Lucille! As mad as I was, I didn't forget what I wanted to do.

Lucille saw the spider at the same time I did, but she didn't act a bit scared.

So I grabbed a stick and started yelling, "Look out, Lucille! There's a spider! *It'll bite you!*"

I thought if I could get her really scared, I'd seem more like a hero to her when I killed the spider. So I yelled again, still louder, "Lucille! Quick! Get out of the way! There's a great big, ugly, long-legged spider about to eat you up!"

Well, this is the part of the story I hate to tell anybody, but I may as well get it over with. That helpless girl grabbed the stick out of my hand, which was Little Jim's stick anyway, and she swooped down on that spider and whacked it with the stick and jumped on it with her shoes and killed it herself!

Then she looked at me, disgusted, and said, "Fraidycat! What is there about a dumb old spider to be afraid of? Did you think it was going to bite you?"

Then Lucille threw the stick across the playground, and she and Sylvia and the other girl swished around, gathering up their scattered lunch boxes, and went in the schoolhouse.

After that I was more disgusted with girls than ever, and for some reason I didn't like Bill Collins very well either. Not for a long time.

8

Winter in our country meant a lot of snow and plenty of wind. Snowdrifts were sometimes higher than our heads. We made snow forts in our school yard and had snow battles, all in fun. We even got my coaster wagon and made an armored tank out of it, which we filled full of snow cannonballs and bombs, and we charged on each other like modern armies.

Only we didn't like to play army very well because real war is so terrible and so many people get killed or have to leave their homes. We decided to quit playing war and played other snow games, such as fox and geese. We made snowmen and snow caves and had a lot of fun.

Of course, we did our chores at night, and I kept right on helping Mom with the dishes at different times. I kept on learning to hang up my clothes on a hanger and always to wipe my shoes on a mat outside the door or take off my boots before I went into the house, so our house would look like a house instead of a barn.

All the time Charlotte Ann kept growing fatter and prettier, and Dad kept doing all kinds of antics to get her to smile, such as making funny faces, tickling her chin or cheeks or pink toes, or twisting his bushy blackish-red eyebrows. In November when she was six months old, two little white baby teeth stuck their edges up through the lower gums of her mouth.

Was she ever fussy while those teeth were pushing through! I was as disgusted as anything with her until Mom reminded me that I'd been even fussier when I was little. I was surprised when I heard that, and I didn't like to believe it, but Dad said it was true. So after I'd frowned a while, I quit and forgave Charlotte Ann.

Charlotte Ann's two teeth came through just in time for Thanksgiving dinner—only, of course, she couldn't have any turkey because babies don't eat anything but milk and maybe some ground-up, cooked spinach or fruit or whatever a doctor says to feed them.

That was one of the best dinners I ever had in my life, and I liked it especially well that we'd invited Old Man Paddler to eat with us. My red-haired, freckled-faced city cousin was there too. His dad was my dad's brother. They brought with them their brown-and-tan Airedale dog, Fritz. He was medium sized and had thick, rough hair, which looked like it had never been combed, and short ears.

I could see right away that Fritz and Mixy didn't like each other, and I knew there'd be trouble before the visit was over. Fritz didn't like any cats very well, which most dogs don't.

The day before Thanksgiving, my red-haired, freckled-faced city cousin and I went out to the pen where our big old turkey was locked up, getting fatter and lazier all the time. Fritz was with us. His tail was standing straight up like the tail of the little blue Scottish terrier on Charlotte Ann's bassinet.

Dogs, you know, have at least eight different kinds of tails. There was a book in my library that told about them. You see, my parents had a corner of their library filled with books especially for boys, and I called it *my* library. There was a book on wild animals of America, birds of America, wild flowers and trees, and a large, beautiful Bible storybook, which was easy to read and understand, and many other good storybooks. I guess my parents thought my mind was as important as the rest of me, and they wanted to give it something to eat. They knew it was especially good for a boy to read good books.

Well, one of those books had a short chapter telling all about the different kinds of dogs' tails. The "ring" tail, for example, starts straight up, then curves around over the dog's back, making a complete circle. The "sickle" tail is shaped like the sharp sickle Dad uses to cut weeds. The "whip" tail hangs straight back like the tail of Circus's English setter dog. The "crank" tail hangs like the crank on an old-fashioned car. The "gay" tail stands straight up like Fritz's did and like the tails of Scottish terriers do.

When it rained, our turkey's tail hung down so the rain would run off his back. When he felt proud and liked to show off, he would spread his feathers like a big fan. He could make himself look almost twice as big as he was.

Well, Walford, which is my city cousin's name, and Fritz and I stood looking through the wire fence at Caesar, the turkey. We said different things about him and tried to get him to pay attention to us, which he wouldn't. But once in a while he'd lift his naked reddish head and let out a hideous "Gobble-gobble-obble-obble-obble!" that made Fritz whimper and try to get through the fence so he could play with him.

I was feeling a little sad, knowing that by this time tomorrow old Caesar would be naked all over and without any head or feet and would be lying upside down all full of stuffing in Mom's big oven, getting nice and brown for our dinner. I liked old Caesar, and I think he liked me. Sometimes he would let me pet him.

Everything would have been all right if Walford hadn't been so proud of the different tricks Fritz could do. Pretty soon Walford got tired of just looking at old Caesar so he decided he wanted to tie a rope around the turkey's scrawny neck and teach Fritz to lead him. I knew right away that it wasn't a good idea, but Walford didn't know it and neither did Fritz. I argued against it for a while and then finally gave in and went and got a rope just to show Walford he was wrong.

Then we went into the pen. I fastened one end of the rope to Caesar's neck, while he kept shaking his head at me, not liking it very well.

Walford fastened the other end of the rope to Fritz's collar.

It turned out that Walford was right—with a little coaxing and Walford leading him, Fritz marched around and around inside the fence, leading old Caesar. Fritz was as proud as anything. I even wished I could get on Caesar's back and ride.

Walford laughed and laughed and shouted, "See there! What did I tell you!"

Yes, he was right—for about five minutes—until Fritz spied Mixy on the other side of the gate, which was shut but wasn't hooked. Something inside of me went first cold and then hot. I seemed to know something was going to happen. In fact, it was already happening right before my scared eyes.

The very second that Airedale spied Mixy's black-and-white fur there by the gate, he forgot all about being tied to a turkey's neck. He whirled and made a dash for the gate, where I was standing. Before I could stop him, he shoved it open and gave chase to Mixy—and here came old Caesar squawking and gobbling and flopping after him.

Walford and I screamed at the top of our lungs for Fritz to stop.

But Fritz was like a car going downhill without any brakes.

I couldn't think very well, but I thought, *What if Fritz catches Mixy? He might even kill her!* I made a grab for the rope and missed it.

Then I quick decided to slam the gate shut,

thinking I could catch the rope in the crack between the gate and the post and stop Fritz. I guess I was more worried about saving Mixy than I was Caesar's neck, so without thinking until afterwards, I threw my whole weight against the gate, which was seventy-two pounds, and slammed it hard.

Well, that stopped Fritz. In fact he stopped so quick he almost turned a somersault backwards. Mixy went scooting like a scared rabbit straight for the barn, flashed through a hole under it, and was safe.

But that wasn't all that happened. The gate had shut *ker-squash* right on Caesar's scrawny old neck!

Anyhow, that's how I killed our Thanksgiving turkey that fall. Actually, Dad had to finish killing him, which he did with a sharp ax on a big block of wood.

9

Poetry came over to our house after dinner that day because he'd heard my city cousin was there and he wanted to see Walford. Nearly all our gang had city cousins, and they didn't know much about country life. In fact, the first time Walford came to see me, which was when he was little, he was so ignorant he thought milk grew in bottles on trees like bananas.

As I told you, he had a very freckled face. In fact there wasn't even one tiny corner of his face that didn't have freckles on it. He had two upper front teeth that were too big for his small face. But that didn't matter, because by the time his face quit growing, his teeth would be just the right size. You see, the teeth were already as big as they would ever get. Lots of boys—and even girls—look funny when they're ten years old, and they can't help it.

I could see the minute Poetry came wading through the snow toward us that he was in a mischievous mood. I'd warned Walford ahead of time not to get angry at anything he did or said.

When Poetry got to within about ten feet of us, he stopped and stared at Walford as if he was seeing a ghost. Then he stooped and stretched his neck this way and that and rubbed his eyes as though he was trying to see better or else couldn't believe what he was seeing. He walked all the way around us, looking at Walford as if looking at some interesting animal in a zoo.

Then Poetry stopped, grunted, and looked at Walford's freckles and big front teeth, which were almost far enough apart to push a feather through, and at his red hair, which showed under his winter cap. Then with his eyes still on Walford, he said to him, "What big ears you have, Grandma!" quoting from the story of Little Red Riding Hood and the wolf.

Walford's face turned even redder than it was, but he didn't get mad. He just grinned and said in a deep voice like the old wolf's, "All the more to hear you with, my dear."

And Poetry said, "What big teeth you have, Grandma!"

And Walford said, "All the more to eat you up with, my dear!"

With that remark, Walford looked down at Poetry's feet, which certainly were extra large for a boy Poetry's age, and said, "What big feet you have, Little Red Riding Hood!"

And in a jiffy both boys were in the middle of a good old-fashioned snow fight, neither one of them being angry but each one trying to see which was the stronger, as boys will do.

Fritz came running through the snow and joined in the scramble, and that reminded me of the turkey.

After we'd talked about that incident a while, I told Poetry about Old Man Paddler coming to our house for dinner tomorrow. Poetry's eyes lit up at that because every boy who knew Old Man Paddler liked him. I suppose the reason was because Old Man Paddler just liked kids and was always doing something for them. Kids are sort of like dogs. If you like them and are kind to them, they'll like you and be kind to you.

That started us talking about Old Man Paddler, and Poetry and I had a good time for a while telling Walford about the exciting things that had happened to the Sugar Creek Gang that summer. We told him how we'd found a map hidden in a hollow tree and how we had caught a robber at midnight while he was digging for Old Man Paddler's money in the swamp, and how Little Jim had killed a fierce mother bear—things like that.

Then like thunder out of a blue sky, Walford asked, "What became of Old Man Paddler's nephew, who got shot when the police thought he was a robber?"

We had actually forgotten all about him. In fact, after he'd gotten out of the hospital, he had just disappeared, and we hadn't seen or heard of him since.

"He'll get all Old Man Paddler's money when the old man dies, won't he?" Walford asked.

That made me remember that the kind old man had told the Sugar Creek Gang that he'd put something in his will for every one of us. But that was a secret. Nobody else was to know, so I said to Walford, "I guess Barry Boyland"—

which is the nephew's name—"is the only living relative."

Poetry winked at me secretly, and we started talking about something else, but not until Walford had said, "I wonder how the old man gets his groceries and things in the winter when the snow is too deep for him to go to town?"

And that's what our gang was wondering that day in the middle of December when we packed Poetry's sled with supplies and went up to see him. But I'll have to tell you about Thanksgiving dinner first, when Old Man Paddler ate with us.

Thanksgiving Day came at last, and we were all sitting around the table at our house: Uncle Phil, Aunt Bessie, Mom, Dad, Charlotte Ann, Walford, me—and dear Old Man Paddler, who had the best table manners I ever saw. He had on his new glasses, which had thick lenses, and he always wore them when he was reading or eating and had to see things up close. Most of the time they were off and in a little brown case in his pocket.

Charlotte Ann was sitting in a high chair, tied in so she wouldn't fall out, and waiting to be fed a bite whenever Mom decided to give one to her. She had on a cute white dress and a blue-and-white bib tied on with strings around her neck. There was a blue stripe running all the way down the middle of the bib.

Walford and I were both in a very mischievous mood, which boys sometimes get into at the wrong times, and not on purpose either.

Just when I was supposed to be quiet because it was time to ask the blessing, I thought of something funny. I felt a smile coming on my face, and I knew I was going to snicker out loud, and I wasn't going to be able to help it.

It was Charlotte Ann's blue-and-white bib that caused it. I looked at Old Man Paddler's long beard, which completely covered his chest like a bib and was as clean as Mom's white tablecloth. Then I thought, *What if he'd accidentally spill some of Mom's blueberry jam on it and it'd run all the way down and make a long blue mark like the blue stripe on Charlotte Ann's bib?*

It wasn't even funny, I guess, but I thought it was, and I giggled out loud just as Dad bowed his head. In fact, he had just said, "Will you ask the blessing first, Bill?"

We nearly always did it that way at our house. I generally prayed a little poem prayer I'd learned. Then Mom or Dad prayed afterward and said something, although we sometimes just bowed our heads and shut our eyes and each one prayed his own prayer quietly without saying any words out loud.

Well, there we all sat with our heads bowed and with Old Man Paddler's white whiskers almost touching my blushing cheeks, and I was supposed to pray!

Things looked bad for me, but I knew I hadn't done wrong *on purpose* and that God knew I was a boy and He liked boys as well as anybody. So I pinched myself hard on the leg so I wouldn't snicker again, and it hurt so much I said "Ouch" instead. I would have snickered again, but I felt Dad's eyebrows hanging over me, so I quoted my poem prayer:

"We thank Thee, Father, for our homes.
For friends who help each day,
For food we eat and clothes we wear,
For all the gifts Thy children share."

And at that very minute I remembered that I'd planned to surprise my parents by adding some words of my own next time I prayed, so I said, "We thank You also for Jesus, our Savior, who died for us. And help us to always live for Him. Amen."

Then Old Man Paddler prayed a beautiful prayer, thanking the Lord for different things such as a country that was free from war and things like that. And then he prayed for all our gang by name, not by our real names either but by the names we had mostly given each other: Big Jim, Little Jim, Circus, Dragonfly, Poetry, and Bill, which was me.

When I opened my eyes and looked up, I didn't feel like snickering anymore. I could feel both Mom and Dad looking at me, and I knew they were wondering if I was all right or maybe just a little off in my mind or something.

Old Man Paddler was looking at me too with the kindest eyes, as if he liked me very much. I could hardly see his eyes though, unless I looked around the edges of his glasses, on account of the lenses being so thick.

Late that afternoon I was alone up in our haymow throwing down hay for our horses and cows. I was remembering something important my dad had taught me once: When you know you've done something wrong—even if you didn't do it on purpose—if you confess it to God right away, He'll forgive you that very minute. So while I was standing on a great big mound of hay, I prayed and told my heavenly Father that I didn't laugh at prayer time on purpose but I knew it was wrong anyway and that I was sorry.

There wasn't any answer out loud, but I knew way down inside of me that everything was all right, and that He still liked me. So I started singing a new chorus Sylvia's dad had taught us, which goes like this:

"It's a grand thing to be a Christian,
    It's a grand thing, I know."

And those are all the important things that happened until we went up to Old Man Paddler's cabin, which I'm going to tell you about right now.

10

One cold day our gang went up to see Old Man Paddler, although it wasn't very cold when we started.

Nobody around our neighborhood had seen the old man for a while because the weather had been snowy, so we supposed he had decided to stay in and keep warm. We knew he had plenty of wood to burn because, as I told you, there was a great big high stack right in the main room of his cabin, and there was another little room that was almost full of wood too.

But even an old man had to eat, so our gang, with our parents saying we could, decided to take Poetry's big toboggan full of groceries and go up to the log cabin in the hills where the old man lived to pay him a visit. A toboggan, you know, is a sled that generally doesn't have any runners but is made of long, flat, thin boards curved up at the front end.

Dad went to town the morning of that day, which was Saturday, and got the old man's mail. There were a half dozen letters (one from California) and two new magazines that the old man subscribed to. So we took the letters and magazines with us, knowing they'd help to make us welcome.

The sky was clear and as blue as one of my

mom's summer morning glories when we started. Each one of us wore snowshoes, which look something like tennis rackets. When you have snowshoes on, you don't have to go around snowdrifts if you don't want to but can walk right on top of them and not sink in.

Pretty soon we had Poetry's toboggan packed and were ready to go. Each one of our mothers had given us something to take, such as bread and butter; tin cans of milk, corn, and beans; bacon; and flour. Little Jim's mother sent some sassafras roots for making sassafras tea, which was Old Man Paddler's favorite drink—and Little Jim's too, ever since he'd learned how good it was.

It was about one o'clock in the afternoon when we started. We decided to follow the old wagon trail that winds around among the hills, getting higher and higher all the time. Years ago, our folks told us, before Old Man Paddler had taken his trip around the world and was gone so long everybody thought he was dead, the road had been pretty good. He had owned a horse and wagon then, which he drove to town and back. The road was still there, but it wasn't used anymore, and in some places fallen trees lay across it.

There were a lot of deep snowdrifts in it that day. But we decided to follow it anyway so we'd be sure not to get lost, although Poetry had a compass on one end of his waterproof matchbox.

The compass looked a little like a watch,

only instead of having numbers on its face as watches do, it had letters: N for north; S for south; E for east; and W for west. A lot of letters, which told you exactly which direction was which, were in between. Instead of having two hands as watches do, the compass had just one, and it always pointed straight north, so you could always know which direction you were going.

On the other end of Poetry's waterproof matchbox was a magnifying glass called a "burning glass," which first-class Boy Scouts know how to use to start a fire when they don't have matches. And between the compass and the magnifying glass was a place for matches. Poetry always carried his matchbox with him whenever we went on important trips, so we'd have a compass and not get lost. And we were always needing matches.

The only thing wrong with a winter day when the sun shines down on you and the snow looks like a big white blanket spread all over the ground—and in some places the wind has made the snowdrifts look like big waves of white water—is that you keep wishing it wasn't so cold so you could go swimming.

Big Jim and Circus walked on ahead, pulling the toboggan, doing what is called "breaking trail," which means finding the best places to walk and walking there themselves so it would be easier for Little Jim and the rest of us to follow.

Dragonfly was just learning how to use

snowshoes. Sometimes he would forget to lift the forward end of his foot before trying to take the next step, which is about the same as trying to step up on the curb when you're in town without lifting your foot. If you don't lift your foot first, *ker-squash* you go, headfirst in a snowdrift, which Dragonfly did maybe a dozen times until he started to remember to lift his foot first. The first time he fell in, we had to help him out because the drift was so deep. Sometimes you can't get out at all without kicking your snowshoes off first.

We laughed at Dragonfly, and Poetry teased him by saying:

"Humpty Dumpty sat on a wall,
  Humpty Dumpty had a great fall;
  All the king's horses and all the king's men
  Couldn't put Humpty Dumpty together again."

Then, just about a minute later, Poetry forgot to lift *his* foot first, and *swaddle-de-dump-ker-sizzle,* down he went headfirst into a huge, very soft drift. There he was completely buried with his snowshoes kicking. And he couldn't get up or out until we helped him.

Big Jim stopped and came back to where we were. With all of us helping, we dragged Poetry back by the legs to a place where the snow wasn't so deep—Dragonfly said it was like dragging a hippopotamus.

Then, before Poetry could get up, Dragonfly—who was still disgusted with him for calling him Humpty Dumpty—pointed at him and yelled, "Look, gang! This is the cow with the crumpled horn, that tossed the dog, that worried the cat, that caught the rat, that ate the mat, that lay—"

Poetry rolled over quick and grabbed Dragonfly by the leg. Down Dragonfly went again.

Well, a wrestling match in a snowdrift, with snowshoes on, is fun to watch, so we watched until Big Jim stopped it and said we'd better go on.

It was a lot farther following the wagon trail than taking the shortcut through the swamp that we took in the summertime. But of course it was safer, and it's silly for a boy to run any foolish risks just because he isn't afraid to. Dad says that being brave isn't half as important as having good sense.

It was half past two by Big Jim's watch when we came to the spring where the old man got his water, which was about half a city block's distance from the cabin.

"Look!" Dragonfly cried. "There aren't any footprints or any path coming down to the spring."

The snow was very deep there too. It had snowed hard last night, I thought, so maybe the old man hadn't shoveled a path yet because he had enough water in the house to last him for the day.

"Here we go!" Big Jim shouted back to us. "Let's shovel a big wide path for him!"

Then Dragonfly yelled again, "There isn't any smoke coming out of his chimney either!"

Without knowing why, I began to feel very weird inside. I remembered what the kind old man had said one day last summer when we'd told him we hoped he'd live forever. He had laughed and said, "Live forever? That's exactly what I'm going to do, only I'm going to move out of this dilapidated old house first."

And we knew he didn't mean his weathered old log house with its clapboard roof, which looked like a picture of the house Abraham Lincoln was born in. He meant a wrinkled, white-haired house with long white whiskers and gnarled old hands that trembled.

We hurried around to where we could see the front door. Poetry, who had run on ahead, let out an excited gasp and squawked, "Look, everybody! The door's wide open, and the floor's all covered with snow!"

Poetry was right. A big drift was right inside the door, and snow was all over.

For a minute not one of us said a word. I thought, *What if he's already dead?* We stood looking at each other sad-like, as people do when they stand around in front of a church after a funeral, waiting for the pallbearers to come walking down the steps with the casket.

Then Big Jim said, "You boys wait a minute."

My teeth were chattering, and it couldn't have been because I was cold, because walking with snowshoes on will make you warm quicker than you can get warm standing around a fire, unless it's terribly cold. It *was* getting colder, but I think my teeth must have been chattering because I was afraid the old man was dead.

Little Jim had a very sad expression on his face.

We watched Big Jim go up to the open door. He took off one of his heavy mittens and gave four sharp raps with his knuckles and waited, while I kept on holding my breath and feeling half scared and half excited. You know you ought never to walk into anybody else's house or even into his room without knocking first. Mom says it's a "law of etiquette" that has to be obeyed if you want to be polite.

Big Jim knocked again, listened, and didn't hear anything. When he knocked the third time and nobody answered, he called, "Hello! Anybody home?"

Still there was no answer. So he called back to us, "There's nobody here!"

We decided we'd better go in to see what was wrong, although there was already a sad picture in my mind of what we might find when we got inside. I could imagine the old man lying there on the cot with his clean white whiskers covering his whole chest, and maybe his eyes would be shut, and he would be dead. Or maybe he was already buried under the snow that had drifted in through the open door, there having been a very hard wind last night.

I put my arm around Little Jim so he wouldn't shake so—and maybe so I wouldn't shake so much either.

"I'm not s-scared. I'm just c-cold," he said bravely.

I guess that was the first time I'd noticed how *much* colder it was up here in the hills than it had been at home. It felt almost twice as cold, although the sun was still shining and that helped some. There weren't any clouds in the sky except maybe two or three big white ones that looked like a lot of cotton balls piled together.

Big Jim stepped out of his snowshoes and stood them up just outside the cabin door, scooped about eight inches of snow off the step, and started to go in. Then he stopped dead still and straightened up with a jerk and listened again.

I guess we'd all heard it at once, whatever it was. It sounded like the wind moaning in the trees, which it might have been, because the wind was beginning to blow a little. We all kept on listening, and we didn't hear anything else, so pretty soon we were all inside the main room where the fireplace was.

But Old Man Paddler wasn't there. The cot over in the corner where he slept was empty. There was a pile of wood but no fire. Poetry and Dragonfly hurried into the other room of the cabin to see if he was there, and he wasn't.

That other room was like our woodshed at home. Along the walls were more stacks of wood—heavy logs for the fireplace and short, split wood for the cookstove.

Back in the main room, we all stood beside the big snowdrift, which we'd been walking on and which was mashed down with our tracks. We kept looking at each other and feeling foolish because we'd thought we heard somebody calling, and yet there wasn't anybody here.

"I'm sure I heard somebody," Poetry said, and Dragonfly said the same thing, and so did I.

"I guess it was the wind in the trees," Big Jim decided, and most of us decided the same thing.

"Where do you suppose he w-went?" Little Jim wanted to know.

Poetry, having a detective mind, began to look around for a note.

Circus said, "Maybe he went to town to get his mail and hasn't come back yet."

"How'd the door get open?" Dragonfly wanted to know.

Poetry said, "The wind, of course."

Everybody was talking, and nobody was listening to anybody, the way grown-up people do sometimes when there are a lot of them together.

I kept thinking, *I'm sure I heard a voice!*

Then suddenly I felt cold chills running all the way up my spine to my red hair, which tried to stand up under my cap but couldn't. I jumped as though somebody had exploded a firecracker behind me, for as plain as day I heard it again, a kind of low moan. And it was right under where I was standing, which was all covered with snow.

11

You could have knocked us all over with a turkey feather! Big Jim whirled around as quick as a baseball player does when he tries to knock a home run and misses the ball. Little Jim's face turned almost as white as the snow he was standing on. Circus looked up at one of the beams that went across from one side of the cabin to the other, as if he thought he'd heard something up there. Dragonfly's eyes were nearly popping out of his head.

Poetry was the only one who seemed to be thinking straight. But he had a sort of detective mind. As quick as a hummingbird can flash from one flower to another, he was down on his knees, scooping away the snow. In a minute he had uncovered a steel ring that was fastened to the floor by a big staple!

We helped him scrape away a lot more snow and saw that somebody had cut a door in the floor, which meant that maybe there was a cellar down there. One side of the trapdoor was covered with pieces of wood—it looked like some of the woodpile had tumbled over and fallen on it. At first we'd thought the split logs were just lying there on purpose.

But how'd a cellar get there? We'd been to the cabin many times last summer, sometimes with Little Jim's bear, and there hadn't been any cellar then.

But I remembered that day about six months before, just as we were leaving, that the old man had stood up and said, "I must be getting on with my work now." He hadn't told us what his work was, and even though we had wanted to ask him, we hadn't because we thought maybe it wasn't any of our business.

All of a sudden Circus remembered something too. "Remember the big rug he always kept here?"

And we remembered. *That's* why we'd never seen the trapdoor before.

Well, here it was—a door cut in the board floor with one hinge showing and the other covered up with a big pile of wood. On one side was the big metal ring, like that kind of door always has, so that you can lift it up when you want to.

Then we heard the moan again, and we knew that somewhere down there was somebody who needed help. When a gang of boys knows somebody needs help, it doesn't take them long to start doing something. In less time than it takes to tell it, we had that pile of wood moved and leaning against a corner of the fireplace, and we were looking down into a big hole under the cabin that looked as black as a barrel of tar. There was a stairway going down, but we couldn't see very well.

"Hello, down there!" Big Jim called, while

Little Jim's hand held on to mine so tight it almost hurt me.

Then somebody answered, with a sad groan. "He-hello!" It was Old Man Paddler's quavery voice.

Knowing he was alive made me feel better. Little Jim sighed loudly, as if somebody had given him a breath of fresh air. I looked at him quick, and I don't know what made me think of it, but I thought his face looked like the face of one of the lambs in my Bible story book. Jesus was carrying the lamb in His arms, and it wasn't afraid.

Big Jim and Circus, being the oldest boys in our gang, went down into the cellar first, walking down a narrow wooden stairway. Then Big Jim called for me to come too.

It wasn't much of a cellar, but it was a good place to keep things in the winter so they wouldn't freeze. Right away I saw Old Man Paddler on the dirt floor, half lying down and half sitting up. He was shivering with the cold. And one of his feet was twisted and swollen as though it had been sprained or broken.

In my mind it was as plain as day what had happened. He had started down to get something. Then he'd slipped on the stair and fell and broke or sprained his ankle and couldn't get back up right away. The wind was blowing hard last night. Maybe it had burst open the outer door of the cabin, which might not have been shut tight. Maybe the door bumped against the trapdoor, which was leaning open against the corner of the fireplace, and the trapdoor fell shut. Maybe all that jarred the high rick of wood along the wall, and it had fallen down on top of the trapdoor. So the old man couldn't get out.

Later we found out that was exactly what had happened.

Well, we had to act fast because Old Man Paddler was suffering, and he was so cold. *He's probably been here all night and all day today,* I thought.

He tried to talk, but his voice was so hoarse we couldn't hear him very well. It sounded as though he said, "Get a fire started and get me in bed quick."

We knew he was right. He seemed to have a bad cold, and even an ordinary cold is dangerous if you don't take care of yourself. Doctors say that even boys ought to go to bed when they have a *bad* cold, because if they do, they can get well twice as quick. And when the doctor says to go to bed and you don't, you might even get pneumonia.

Well, with Old Man Paddler having such a bad cold and maybe a fever, and his being very old, he might get pneumonia too.

We went to work like a nestful of ants. Big Jim told us what to do, and we did it as quick as we could. The first thing we did was to help Old Man Paddler up the stairs, take his shoes off, and get him covered up in bed. *It's a good thing he has long whiskers,* I thought, *because they helped keep his chest warm.*

There were a lot of things that had to be done. We had to start two fires, one in the fireplace and the other in the cookstove. We had to get some water from the spring because all the water in the house was frozen and wouldn't melt quick enough to get him a drink. He had to have one right away because he was very thirsty. We had to get some canned beef and vegetable soup from the toboggan, because a sick man has to have food that is easy to digest.

Circus and Dragonfly went to the spring for water. Little Jim stood close to Old Man Paddler's bed and tried to get his knotty old hands warm by holding them in his and rubbing them under the covers. Poetry pulled the toboggan inside and started to unpack it. And all the time it seemed to be getting colder and colder.

Big Jim and I laid the fire in the fireplace the way Boy Scouts do. We hurried as fast as we could because we had to have hot water for the old man's sprained ankle, and he was still shivering. All the time, while I was doing exactly what Big Jim said, I kept thinking, *What if he gets pneumonia? What if we didn't get here soon enough?*

First, Big Jim wrinkled up some dry paper, and on top of it he put some little twigs and split sticks about half as big as a pencil, which I cut for him with the knife I'd found along Sugar Creek. My fingers were so cold they were getting numb. I'd never seen weather get cold so fast in my life.

All around and on top of the little sticks we

put some broken, middle-sized sticks. I always did like to watch Big Jim start a fire. First there would be a baby fire, which crackled and sizzled, and the little flames would shoot up like hungry yellow tongues begging for more wood to eat. It always made me think of Mom feeding Charlotte Ann, who would sit in her bassinet or in a chair and wait for the next bite, like the baby fire waiting for us to feed it another stick of wood.

Pretty soon Big Jim straightened up and looked around and said to Old Man Paddler, "Where are the matches?" just as Circus and Dragonfly came in from the spring with a kettle of water. Their faces were as red as a red sunset on account of the cold, and there was ice frozen on the outside of the kettle where it had splashed over—it was that cold. They said they had even had to chop a hole through the ice at the spring to get the water.

Then Big Jim sent Poetry, Dragonfly, and Circus out to shovel the snow away from the door and to make a path down to the spring so it'd be easier to get more water when we needed it.

I guess Old Man Paddler hadn't heard Big Jim's question about the matches, so we asked him again.

The old man sat up in bed and nodded to a shelf above the table where there was a matchbox.

I hurried to get the box, and Big Jim opened it and looked in.

"It's empty," he said, and I thought his voice sounded kind of hollow.

Old Man Paddler tried to raise himself up again. "There's another box on the end of the shelf, I think." Then he sank back against the pillow and groaned a little, and I knew we'd have to hurry to get the room warm, or he'd be very sick.

I looked on the shelf, and Big Jim looked, and Little Jim looked. And there wasn't any matchbox! *What if we can't get a fire started at all?* I thought. *We'll all freeze to death!*

Finally, after we'd all three looked everywhere the old man told us to and still couldn't find any matches, I happened to remember Poetry's waterproof matchbox, so I ran to the door and yelled, "Hey, Poetry! Come here. Quick!"

Poetry, who was shoveling snow very fast— to keep warm, I guess—straightened up, and in a fourth of a jiffy he and Dragonfly and Circus all came puffing in.

"What's the matter?" Poetry asked, looking from one to the other and at the little wigwam of sticks and paper in the fireplace.

"Give me your waterproof matchbox quick!" Big Jim commanded.

"Sure!" Poetry said. He put the end of his right mitten between his teeth, pulled his hand out, and shoved it into his coat pocket. I remembered his matchbox had a compass on one end and a burning glass on the other, so in case you ever ran out of matches, you could start a fire with the glass—that is, if the sun was shining, which it still was that very minute. The place for matches was in the middle.

All of a sudden Poetry's face took on a scared expression. He bit off the other mitten and began to run his short, fat hands into every pocket he had—his four pants pockets, two in front and two behind, and all his coat pockets.

And there wasn't any matchbox there! "I-I can't find it!" Poetry puffed.

I knew he must have lost it a half mile down the hill when he had fallen in the snowdrift—where he and Dragonfly had their wrestling match.

12

No matches! No magnifying glass!

That meant there'd be no fire. And it was getting colder all the time.

Just that minute Old Man Paddler coughed as though his cold was already going down into his chest.

We ought to get a doctor, I thought, and I knew it'd take us an hour and a half in the snow to get to a telephone and that whoever came would have to come on snowshoes, and that would take another hour and a half. It'd be dark before then. And with the wind beginning to blow, the snow would move like white dust on a dirt road when a car whizzes past. Even with a light, the doctor couldn't see the way.

Big Jim opened the door and looked out at the thermometer hanging there. Then he shut the door quick and said, "It's below zero already."

That was a lot colder than it had been at home.

For a minute, which seemed like an hour, we stood looking at each other, none of us saying anything.

I glanced over at Little Jim, feeling especially sorry for him because he was so little. Also maybe I looked at him because he was such a good Christian and I thought that pretty soon maybe he'd say something about God that'd make us feel better.

When a boy is in trouble and doesn't have his parents with him, he isn't quite as brave as he is most of the time, and he wishes he was a better Christian—if he is one. And if he isn't, he wishes he was, because as Sylvia's father had said just last Sunday, it's silly not to be a Christian. If you aren't, you won't know how to pray, and, if you should happen to die, then you'd be lost forever.

Do you know that Little Jim's face wasn't scared at all? It was as still and quiet as the face of the lamb Jesus carried in His arms in that picture in my Bible storybook.

It was Dragonfly who surprised us by saying, "Why don't we get down on our knees and pray?"

Well, why don't we? I thought. Of course, when a boy is in danger it is not always good to *stop* and pray. If there was a mad bull chasing a boy, it'd be silly to *stop* and pray. But he could pray on the run—and I'll bet he would too.

Now that I think of it, I guess I'd been praying in my mind ever since I knew Old Man Paddler was down in the cellar needing our help.

We knew God wouldn't send any matches right down out of heaven, but He might help us find a match if there was one. In a jiffy there we all were, down on our knees beside Old Man Paddler's bed.

Dragonfly's prayer was awful short because he was just learning how to pray out loud. I knew just what he was thinking about when he said in a tearful voice, "And if I don't see my p-parents again, I hope they'll get saved before they die."

I looked up for a second when he said that and saw the sun shining through the frost-covered window on the top of his cap. It was so cold none of us had thought to take his cap off, as you are supposed to do when you pray. But I think God knew how cold it was, and He always looks on the heart anyway, Mom says.

That prayer meeting wasn't more than three minutes long, and yet it must have been long in another way, because it was long enough for our prayers to reach all the way to heaven and back again. Suddenly there was what looked like an answer, right in front of our eyes!

As we got up from our knees, Old Man Paddler whispered for me to bring his Bible and his glasses, while the other boys kept looking for that extra box of matches that was supposed to be there and wasn't.

Well, I got the Bible, which was as worn on the inside as it was on the outside. It was while I was helping him put his glasses on that an idea came to me. It just swooped down on me like a chicken hawk swoops down on a little chicken in our barnyard in the summertime! There was our answer to prayer as plain as day!

I could hardly believe it at first, for fear it wasn't so—and maybe the idea *wouldn't* work—but the lenses in the old man's glasses were as thick as a magnifying glass! In fact, that is what they were. They made everything look bigger so he could see to read.

I was so excited I didn't even wait to hear the Bible verse the old man was going to read. "Look, Big Jim!" I almost screamed. "Look! Here's a magnifying glass! I'll bet you can start a fire with *it!*"

Poetry looked at me as if he thought I was crazy, but I knew I was right—I hoped. I'd sat close to Old Man Paddler at our Thanksgiving dinner, and I had noticed how thick the lenses were. And because I'm going to be a doctor someday—maybe an eye doctor—I'd noticed them especially. I'd even borrowed them after dinner that day and read a little, just to see how things looked with them on.

Well, it was our last chance. If we didn't hurry, the sun would go down over the hill or else go behind clouds and stay there. We knew there wouldn't be any use to go back to look for Poetry's matchbox, because it'd be like looking for a needle in a haystack.

In a little while Big Jim was busy trying to start a fire using the glasses. He held one lens over his hand first to see if it would burn. He knew just how to get the sunlight focused. Pretty soon there was a little round spot of light on his hand about the size of a pearl, just like a magnifying glass makes, and Big Jim said, "Ouch!" and jerked his hand away. It had actually been so hot it had burned him!

He whittled some thin shavings from a very dry piece of wood. Then he added some tissue paper, which had been wrapped around a present Little Jim's mom had sent along with us on the toboggan.

We all stood around shivering and standing close to each other to keep warm.

Big Jim laid his pile of shavings and the tissue paper on the lid of an old box, and then we held the door open a crack so he could get the direct sunlight. "As soon as I get a blaze," he said, "I'll carry it to the fireplace, and pretty soon we'll all be warm."

It was easy to say, but it was harder to do.

In a few minutes, I saw a little curl of smoke rise from the piece of tissue paper. Dragonfly gasped and crowded in closer. I looked around quick at Old Man Paddler. His eyes were shut, and his lips were moving, which meant maybe he was praying. I knew he was, in fact. I thought, *What if Bill Collins was Old Man Paddler lying there like that, and some boys were trying to save my life? I'd do what he was doing too.*

When I looked back again at Big Jim, a hole was burned through the paper, but there wasn't any blaze. And all the shavings did was smoke a little and go out.

Poetry, who had a good mind, said, "I'll bet if we had some kerosene, it'd burn."

We looked around and found an old-fashioned kerosene lamp on the mantel above the fireplace.

And now Old Man Paddler lay there breathing kind of hard and with his eyes shut, as if he was very sick or else had gone to sleep.

It didn't take Big Jim long to get the glass

lamp chimney off and the lamp open. He twisted a piece of paper into a little roll, pushed it down into the kerosene, and a minute later he had one of the lenses focusing the sunlight on the tip end of the kerosene-soaked paper.

I kept on shivering and hoping and thinking about my parents. We could all see our breath coming out of our noses and mouths like gray smoke coming out of a house with six chimneys.

"It won't work," Big Jim said, shaking his head and laying the glasses down on the table. Then he put on his mittens and flapped his arms around his sides and slapped his hands against his legs to make the blood circulate better so he could get warm. The kerosene-soaked paper was even worse than plain paper. All it did was smoke.

Big Jim stopped flapping his arms, took a deep breath, and sighed as he let it out. His breath almost hid his face for a minute, like tobacco smoke does a man who smokes.

There was a sudden sound from behind us. Old Man Paddler made a noise as if he was waking up and wanted to say something.

"If you had some dry, decayed wood," he whispered, his husky voice mixed up with his whisper, "you could start a fire." Then he shut his eyes and shivered and seemed to go to sleep again, which I think he did.

"He's right," Big Jim said, "but there isn't any in the cabin."

"I saw some once in a hollow tree right by the old swimming hole," Dragonfly said.

"There ought to be a hollow tree around

here somewhere," Circus said. "I'll go look for one."

"I'll go with you," I said, but Big Jim said no, he'd go himself.

Little Jim wanted to go, but he wouldn't let him either.

So Big Jim took Old Man Paddler's hatchet, and he and Circus went out into the snow, where it was even colder than it was inside, to look for a hollow tree that might have in it some very dry, decayed wood, which is called "punk."

The snow had already begun to drift because of the wind, and that meant that pretty soon, even if the sun was still shining, the blowing snow would be almost as bad as clouds, and we *had* to have sunlight or we couldn't start a fire!

I got to thinking about Mom and Dad and Charlotte Ann and wishing I'd been a better boy. I wished that right that very minute my great big dad would come walking through the door with a box of matches and his strong voice would say, "Hello, everybody! We'll have a roaring fire in just about a minute!"

There wasn't any use to wish that, I knew, but I kept on wishing anyhow.

I kept looking out the little hole where I'd wiped the frost off the window. I had to keep doing it, or it would frost over again. It was so cold and getting colder all the time. I couldn't see very much except the trees—and the snow, which looked like the baby powder Mom uses on Charlotte Ann. It kept blowing like white dust, with the wind picking it up and whirling it from one snowdrift to another, the way a little whirlwind does in the summertime when it picks up dust from the road and carries it out across the cornfield. The sun was still shining though, and I knew that if they'd find some punk pretty soon it still wouldn't be too late. If only they *could* find some!

It seemed Circus and Big Jim never would come back. After they'd been gone for maybe ten minutes, which felt like an hour, I made Dragonfly and Little Jim lie down on a blanket I found in a corner. Then I wrapped it around them and went to look out the window of the other room.

I couldn't see anything of Circus or Big Jim back there, but I thought I did see a big hollow tree. It might have some punk in it! I decided to go out and look. First, I told Dragonfly and Little Jim to lie still, which they promised to do.

I tell you it was cold, and it was very hard walking with those clumsy snowshoes on. I struggled as hard as I could, afraid any minute I might forget to lift my foot and I'd go down in a big drift and not be able to get out. And that is exactly what happened.

The first thing I knew I was down in a huge drift that was as deep as I was tall. I couldn't get out without kicking my snowshoes off, and I couldn't seem to get them off. Big Jim and Circus weren't anywhere in sight, and they couldn't have heard me holler for help anyway on account of the wind. I thought maybe I might not ever get out.

While I was wallowing in that snowdrift like a black bear wallowing in the mud in a swamp, I made a promise to God. "If You'll let me live, and Old Man Paddler, and all the Sugar Creek Gang, I'll try to be the best soldier in the gospel army any boy can be. I'll always be kind to my mother, even when she tells me to do something I don't want to do, and . . ."

Then I called for help as loud as I could, but nobody heard me. The wind on my face felt like a lot of little arrows were shooting me with icicles as sharp as needles.

After what seemed like a terribly long time, I began to get sleepy and didn't even want to get up, which is how you feel when you're about to freeze to death. If you do lie down and go to sleep and nobody finds you, maybe you *will* freeze. So be sure never to give up when you're out in a snowstorm and begin to feel sleepy. Keep on working or walking, because that'll help get you warm.

But I didn't know that then, so I just let myself give up, and I lay there as if I was going to bed in a great big feather bed. Pretty soon I'd wake up in heaven maybe.

The next thing I knew, Big Jim and Circus were making me stand up and walk, which I did without wanting to, being even disgusted with them for making me.

"Come on!" Big Jim gasped, pulling me by one arm and Circus pulling me by the other. "We've found some punk, and we'll have a fire in no time!"

13

Pretty soon we were back in the cabin, where there wasn't any wind. I saw that Old Man Paddler still had his eyes shut and seemed to be asleep.

As soon as Big Jim could, he focused the sunlight on that little reddish-brown piece of decayed wood they'd found. The punk was as light as a piece of paper and could be crushed in your hand almost as easily as a cracker could.

Almost the second that round spot of concentrated sunlight touched that punk, it began to smoke. Big Jim's hands trembled a little because he was so cold. He had to brace his hand against the door to keep it steady.

Right away there was more and more smoke. Then I saw a red glow of fire about the size of a pinhead, which grew bigger as Big Jim blew on it. He kept on holding the spot of light on the same place, moving it around a little so the fire would spread. His face was very serious.

"Get me a piece of tissue paper!" he ordered through his teeth. Then he held the roll of tissue against the red coal and blew on it, and kept on blowing, making the red coal bigger and making more smoke.

I tell you I felt like shouting, for right there before our eyes a yellow tongue of flame shot up, and there was our fire!

It didn't take Big Jim long to carry that tiny paper torch over to the little wigwam of sticks in the fireplace. From then on we were just like a bunch of noisy blackbirds, all of us feeding the baby fire a small stick whenever Big Jim would let us. Soon there was a roaring blaze that made us feel mighty good.

We started another fire in the cookstove, boiled some water, made sassafras tea, heated beef and vegetable soup for Old Man Paddler, and put hot wet towels on his swollen ankle.

You should have seen that old man brighten up! As soon as it was warm in the cabin, he let us prop him up in bed. And when the soup was ready, Poetry, who had seasoned it because he was the best cook of any us, carried a great big steaming bowlful to him.

Before he ate, his hoarse voice whispered, "I think we ought to be thankful, boys," and in a second he closed his eyes for prayer. He couldn't bow his head very well because he was leaning back against the pillow we had put there for him. But he nearly always prayed with his face looking up anyway.

It was awful quiet while we waited for him to begin. I could hear the wind outside, whirring around the cabin, the fire roaring in the cookstove, and the blaze crackling and sizzling in the fireplace.

I tell you that was a grand prayer. First he thanked God for answering our prayers. Then he thanked Him for the Sugar Creek Gang, calling us all by our nicknames as he always did. He finished by saying, "And bless Little Tom Till and Bob Till and all the boys in the world who don't have Christian parents to take them to Sunday school and church and teach them to love Jesus and live right. Help all the Christian pastors and schoolteachers and senators and congressmen and all the leaders of our country to do something about saving our boys. And help the leaders in other countries not to forget the millions of boys that are living all around them. Help the parents especially . . ."

For some reason, while the old man was praying, I began to like my mom and dad better than ever and to be very proud of them. I wished that right that minute I could go running lickety-sizzle from the kitchen of our house into the living room and make a dive for my mom and dad and give them a great big hug. I do that sometimes when I happen to see them standing together somewhere, hugging each other the way parents do. Then I wished I could scoop little Charlotte Ann up in my arms and hold her curly head with its soft cheeks and pug nose up against my freckled face and give her a hug too.

It was while Old Man Paddler was eating his soup that Little Jim remembered the mail, which was one of the reasons we had come up there in the first place.

Old Man Paddler took the letters one at a time in his wrinkled hands, holding them up close to his eyes and looking at them through his thick glasses. I didn't like it very well that he had to wear glasses, because I liked to see his kind old eyes twinkle, and I couldn't because of the glasses. And he had so many whiskers that you couldn't tell whether he was smiling unless you saw his eyes.

With the cabin nice and warm and with Old Man Paddler feeling better and maybe not going to be very sick at all—except that he couldn't walk on his sprained ankle and would have to stay in bed for a while till it got well and until his cold was better—and with all of us drinking sassafras tea, we forgot about how cold it was outside.

We boys were sitting around the fireplace, just thinking and talking and feeling cheerful, when the old man surprised us by saying, "I suppose you boys remember my nephew, Barry Boyland, who was shot last summer?"

We'd nearly forgotten about him. In fact, I hadn't thought about him more than once, and that was when my city cousin, Walford, had asked about him the day we accidentally killed our old Thanksgiving turkey. (That crazy, ignorant Airedale dog! He should have had more sense than to try to chase a cat while he was tied to a turkey's neck! But dogs are like that— even stranger than girls who think boys are afraid of spiders, which I'm not.)

Then the old man said something that made us feel sad again. He said, "I've been thinking about the will I made in which I put something for each member of the Sugar Creek Gang."

He stopped talking and turned the letter from his nephew over in his hands. We just sat looking at him and listening to the wind and the fire and waiting for him to talk on.

Pretty soon he did. "It's the Till boys I'm thinking about," he said, "Tom and Bob. I am very glad that Little Tom is going to Sunday school regularly, and I think it is fine the way you boys have been treating Bob, even though he is your enemy. I think I ought to tell you that I'd like to have them in my will too, and they can be if—" Then the old man stopped talking.

I felt an exclamation point rising up out of my head, the way they do in cartoons in the newspaper when people are astonished about something. For a minute I didn't like the idea, because I didn't like Bob Till. I liked little red-haired Tom, but Bob was so wicked, and he said such awful words and hated Sunday school and was so ignorant he thought boys who loved Jesus were sissies!

None of us said anything for a while. In fact, we didn't say anything at all, although I saw Poetry's eyes, and he looked at me disgusted-like. Then I looked at Little Jim, but he still looked like the little lamb I told you about.

Then the old man tore open his nephew's letter, the one from California, and started to read it. But he didn't. There seemed to be something else he wanted to say first. He explained to us what his will said—that anybody who was a member of the Sugar Creek Gang could get in on the will, and it was up to us who we got to join the gang, but that nobody could join unless he wanted to.

"Don't worry about there not being enough for everybody," he said, "because there is."

Then the old man told us one of the most important things in the world. I can't explain it very well even if I do understand it myself. But anybody who wants to have everlasting life and have all his sins forgiven forever and go to heaven can have it—all for nothing—if he'll let Jesus save him.

It's all in the sort of "will" Jesus made when He died. There's enough everlasting life and forgiveness for everybody, and there's plenty of room in heaven, because God owns the whole world and all of heaven and a million stars and planets. And the only thing that'll keep people from getting into God's "will" is their sins, which they won't be sorry for and won't quit doing, and their unwillingness to open the door of their stubborn hearts to let Jesus in.

Well, I certainly liked to hear the kind old man explain things about the Bible, but I knew it was hard for him to talk on account of his cold. Even while he was explaining, though, I was making up my mind to try to get Tom Till into both wills.

I guess I was also thinking about that letter from Barry Boyland, which was lying on the pretty, many-colored Indian blanket on Old Man Paddler's bed. That is, it had been, for just that minute he raised his knees and the letter fell off onto the brown rug beside the bed.

Circus made a dive for the letter and handed it back to the happy old man. He lifted it close to his eyes and began to read.

We could tell the letter had something very interesting in it, because—even though we couldn't see his eyes very well—we could tell by the way his whiskers moved that the letter was making him happy and that there was a smile buried away down there somewhere.

When we found out what the letter said, there were six of the broadest smiles on six of the happiest boys you ever saw. What do you suppose the letter said?

"Will you read it out loud?" the old man asked Big Jim, maybe because he was our leader. He took off his glasses, and about twenty twinkles were in his eyes.

This is what Big Jim read, and what we listened to:

Dear Uncle Seneth,
[that's Old Man Paddler's first name]
    Thank you very much for the check for $1,000 which came yesterday. I think your plan to give the Sugar Creek Gang a vacation next year is a very good one.
    Tell them that I'll be driving past Sugar Creek along about July 5 or 6 next year and to be ready. I haven't decided yet where we'll camp, but it'll be near a lake somewhere. Tell Poetry to have his tent ready because some of the boys will have to sleep in it. They may take turns if they like. Bill will need his binoculars, and each boy will need his New Testament as well as his fish-

ing rod and swimming suit. A warm sweater will come in handy too in case we go up into the north woods where it gets cold at night, even in July.

Perhaps Big Jim ought to bring his rifle, because if we do go up north, there'll be wildcats in the woods that might get a little too friendly . . .

There was more in the letter, but that was all that especially concerned us. Boy oh boy! That was enough, too! Talk about a flock of noisy blackbirds! We were even worse!

Think of a camping trip in the north woods! For two whole weeks next summer! Of course, we'd have to get our parents' permission, but that'd be easy because our parents knew what was good for boys.

Now, I am very sorry to say that I'll have to end this story right here, because it's long enough. I can't even tell you about how we had to stay all night in that cabin because of a terrible blizzard that came up before we could start home. But everything came out all right, even if our parents did worry about us and nearly a dozen men came up in the middle of the night to find out if we were all right.

And even if this story wasn't already long enough, I couldn't tell you about our camping trip because it hasn't happened yet. But just as soon as summer comes, and it's all over, I'll sit right down the very first thing and write about it for you.